GIVING THE DRAGON ICE

VICTORIA JAYNE

Connect with Victoria,

https://www.authorvictoriajayne.com/
https://www.tiktok.com/@authorvictoriajayne
https://www.instagram.com/authorvictoriaj/
https://www.facebook.com/victoria.jayne.7982
https://www.goodreads.com/author/show/18610623.Victoria_Jayne
https://www.bookbub.com/profile/victoria-jayne

DEDICATION

For the real Alisa. Your support of my writing is unmatched. Thank you for all that you do. Booktalk After Dark, you are such an amazing community I am thankful to be a part of you.

1

ALISA ROBERTS

Careful not to stand downwind, Alisa hung around the magazine stand outside the Arach Jewelry building in Manhattan, pretending to struggle with the choice between *Vogue* and *Marie Claire*. Her true intention was to catch a glimpse of her father, Duncan Hayes. If she could summon enough nerve, she might even approach him and introduce herself.

He'd never recognize her. Her father had chosen a different mate over her mother and had been entirely absent from her life. However, she'd always longed to *know* him—not just *of* him. After her mother was murdered when Alisa was nine years old, the need intensified. Now it overwhelmed her.

Anytime she asked about her father, her grandmother spat on the ground. It took twenty years of badgering to even get her to speak his name. Once Alisa learned it, a simple google search revealed quite a bit about him.

Duncan Hayes, the wealthy philanthropist and designer of exquisite fine jewelry, had a lovely enough mate and two sons. Not a bad gig. Dealing with gems was totally something a dragon shifter would do for a living.

Alisa had read numerous articles and scrolled through pages and pages of photos of him at charity galas, rubbing elbows with celebrities. While he was well-off, she wasn't gawking at his wealth. She wasn't even sure she sought any sort of relationship with him. She just wanted an idea of what he looked like and where she came from.

At least, that was what she told herself, standing outside the building he owned. Would he come outside? Had he arrived already? It's possible she might have missed him if he were an early riser. She definitely wasn't. Hell, she hadn't even gone to bed since she left work.

"Hey! This isn't a library," the stand attendant barked. "Either buy something or get moving."

"Oh, right." Alisa stuffed the *Marie Claire* back into its slot. "Sorry about that."

With heated cheeks, she fished in her pocket for her debit card to offer the annoyed man behind the counter. Considering the area, *Vogue* was probably the better choice. Hell, there might even be samples of her father's jewels inside the pages. She couldn't deny he had great taste in jewels—thus, his success.

The man nodded as he swiped the card. Rolling the magazine, she blew out a breath. Someone hadn't had their coffee this morning. Now what could she do to appear inconspicuous while waiting for a glimpse of her dad? People didn't just hang outside of office buildings.

Unless they were begging, she supposed. Then again, not in *this* neighborhood. And while she wasn't dressed in the finest business casual attire, she didn't look slovenly. There'd be no way she could pass for houseless. Now she had to come up with another cover so she wouldn't stand out like a sore thumb.

After glancing to her left and then right, she frowned. Not a bus stop in sight. She couldn't even flip through the magazine, pretending to wait for a ride. With a ball of hopelessness burrowing in her gut, she took in the building Duncan Hayes owned.

Anyone who was anyone in the New York social scene had jewelry from Arach. They were a status symbol.

She, and her sparkle-loving dragon, coveted every piece she'd seen from his company.

Though, as a mere bartender, she'd never be able to afford even the tiniest stud earring. Especially since she'd just relocated to Manhattan. The rent for the smallest studio she could find was absurd, and the prices for something from Arach were astronomical.

Alisa didn't need to meet her dad for money. While she wasn't nearly as well-to-do as him, she survived and wasn't struggling. He didn't owe her a damn thing. She just wanted to *know* one of her parents. She didn't *need* anything from him.

Out of the corner of her eye, she spotted a black luxury SUV pulling up to the curb right in front of her father's building. This had to be him. Who else would arrive in that type of car and park there?

Well. Maybe her half brother? She'd read that he worked alongside Duncan Hayes as a designer.

She licked her bottom lip, and hope sped her heartbeat. One long-lost family member might be enough to take the edge off. Her ribs rattled.

Would it be him, though? Would she finally see her dad in the flesh and not just in magazine and tabloid articles?

Holding her breath, she took a step back. The driver hopped out and trotted around the car to the rear passenger side door. Gods. It was about to happen.

Would he look as refined as he had in the paparazzi photos?

The door opened.

Alisa gulped and rolled the magazine tighter in her hands.

She wasn't ready to actually meet him yet. Nope. It wasn't the right time.

Granted, she came uptown to *see* him, but *meeting* him was a completely different story. That'd mean a conversation. She had to figure out the right words to say. Walking up to him and declaring she was his daughter would go over like a lead balloon. No, she needed something better.

But what?

An elegant man exited the dark Land Rover—just like in the magazine photos she'd studied.

It was him.

Her father stood mere yards from her, buttoning his navy suit jacket.

He was nearly seven feet tall—typical of a male dragon shifter. His obviously tailored attire screamed decadence. She wondered if the wisps of gray at his temples were natural or something he did to blend in with humans. At his height, it'd be hard to accomplish, so every bit helped.

Shifters aged much slower than humans and thus had longer lifespans. It had to do with their enhanced healing abilities. Though, someone as prolific as Duncan Hayes, who mingled with humans constantly, most likely attempted to alter his look to appear as though he matured right along with them.

As he surveyed the sidewalk, he met her gaze briefly.

She froze.

Had he seen her?

Could he tell?

Did he know?

They had the same dark, nearly black eyes. Studying him this close gave her time to consider which of her features she'd inherited from him. It wasn't her nose. His was sharp but not pointed. It complemented his features. However, they shared similar cheekbones and chins.

Even a blind goat could see they were related to one another.

Without a doubt in her mind, she knew—deep in her bones—that was Duncan Hayes. She'd finally encountered her father in person.

Now what?

With an impossible amount of grace, he strode toward the front of his building. He must not have noticed her. Maybe they hadn't actually met gazes. Perhaps he'd looked past her. The idea sunk heavily in her gut.

As a shifter, he had advanced senses. Which meant he would've smelled her. Shifters who were related to one another possessed like notes in their scent. Had she stood upwind, he definitely would've picked up on his kin being near.

She'd done everything to avoid him noticing her, but that didn't change the disappointment blossoming inside her.

Except for that brief glance in her direction, where he probably looked through her rather than at her, he didn't show any signs of recognition. Alisa took a deep breath and tried to stuff the disappointment away and ignore it.

The choice of when and how to approach her father was still hers. She held all the cards and had full control of the situation.

As he disappeared inside the doors, she waited for the tightness to leave her body. Where was the relief?

The weight of her gloom tugged the corners of her mouth south into a deep frown. Sadness bore down and made her shoulders slump.

Telling herself she wasn't ready to *actually* talk to him didn't change the fact she wanted him to sense her. They were *shifters*, and he was her *father*. He *should* have.

Sure, she'd taken precautions and stood downwind, but they were within twenty feet of each other.

Shaking her head at herself, Alisa turned to walk away. This train of thought would go nowhere.

Running her hand along the back of her neck, she scratched the sudden itch. Heat blossomed under her fingernails. Flames scorched through her veins. Her skin prickled as her dragon stretched inside the confines of her mind.

Godsdammit. Not now.

Had it been three months already?

Urgently, she glanced side to side for an escape route. The tattoo she'd gotten from the Ember Witches as a toddler would only offer her so much protection. It wouldn't change the fact that dragons were *enormous creatures*. When she shifted, she needed room. The busy narrow streets of Manhattan couldn't accommodate a full-grown dragon—not at this hour.

With her heart thundering in her chest and her skin blistering, she ducked inside an apartment building as someone walked out. Thankful for her shifter speed, Alisa took the stairs three at a time, racing to the roof.

Pain throttled through her as she craned her neck, begging her inner beast to wait just a few seconds. She had four more flights to go. The stairs couldn't hold the weight of a grown-ass dragon. She'd never fit in the confines of the stairwell.

No. No. No. Slow down.

Reaching for the railing, she turned onto the landing. Cracking vibrated through her arm as her bones broke. She clenched her teeth in agony as her scales erupted. Talons tore through the tips of her fingers.

With her head down and both arms out, she made it. She plowed through the last door and gained access to the roof. Relief combined with the growing pain coursing through her. Taking the final moment of humanness she had, Alisa shimmied out of her clothes. Every fiber in her being broke itself and realigned as the dragon burned through her skin.

Hopefully, the humans of this building had nine-to-five jobs and weren't milling around the roof on a random Tuesday morning. Especially in this neighborhood.

She stumbled as her now scaled legs bulged. Once she hit the ground, she lifted her neck and let out a bloodcurdling shriek as her dragon broke through the last of her mental barriers.

As a female dragon shifter who hadn't been given the Ember Witch elixir of protection, Alisa was at the whim of her heat. Every season, when her fertility was at its peak, her dragon stole her control. The beast had feral needs, and she wanted them fulfilled.

Relegated to the confines of the dragon's mind, Alisa tried to catch her breath. They had gotten to the roof. The beast had enough space. As though to test that theory, the several-ton dragon stretched her massive wings before bellowing out the first of many mating calls.

Alisa would be stuck in darkness until her heat was satisfied, she got knocked up, or she found her mate. So far, she'd been lucky to avoid having an unplanned child. Human contraception, when double or tripled up on, seemed to work to prevent pregnancy.

Her magical tattoo prevented humans from seeing her in this form, but male dragons could still hear her shriek. They'd come from all over to answer it, whether Alisa, the human half, wanted them to or not. After a good shake and a little preening, the beast pushed off and took flight.

The plight of a female dragon shifter shunned by the Ember Witches was Alisa's cross to bear. Apparently, the witches murdering her mom hadn't been enough. They doomed Alisa to suffer through her heat because of the choices her mother made.

Honestly, the punishment didn't fit the crime. Her mom had been a lovesick half-mated female dragon who agonized through an unimaginable pain. She went to the Ember Witches for help, and they denied her. The only thing she wanted was the mate she chose. They could've done something, anything, to relieve her anguish.

Instead, they ended her life and left Alisa to endure a heat that would most certainly never result in a mating.

Dragon shifters were rare. Sometimes, when she summoned, none came. For weeks, she'd cry out to deaf ears. Her true mate, the one who could end her mating agony, had most likely already fallen in battle over a female. She might have even witnessed it on the grounds herself.

It didn't change her biology. She would still cycle through. Her dragon would force her shifts and fly them to the mating grounds, where she'd cry out to him if he existed. There was nothing she could do about it.

2

DECLAN QUINN

Declan losing his wingman to a mate had its upsides. One being, Declan didn't have to listen to Gideon's advice about feline shifters. Second, he didn't have to choose. He could have them both.

Sandwiched between Asiatic and African lioness shifters was the perfect ending to his night on the prowl. Priya, to his right, snaked her hand up his thigh toward his dragon family jewels while nuzzling into his neck. Amani, to his left, teased the outer shell of his ear with her hot breath and warm tongue. Her hand worked the buttons of his shirt. He could die a happy shifter. This was his ultimate fantasy. These beautiful felines could've been drawn from his dreams.

The tiny ruby set in gold in Priya's nose might have gone unnoticed by most, but his dragon loved rubies. They were his favorite gemstone. She would've gotten his attention even if she was alone. The fact she had Amani with her was icing on the cake.

Icing. What could he do with icing and the two gorgeous females?

It'd been a while since he had any cake. If anything warranted confections, a romp with two lionesses definitely did.

"Would you ladies be interested in sweetening this evening?" he asked.

Amani peered at him skeptically. Her light-hazel eyes flicked from him to Priya, but she didn't say a word. It didn't matter the amount of melanin a feline shifter possessed. They all had hazel eyes. When they shifted, the color turned more yellow. It was beautiful to witness. He might even go so far as to say his favorite feline shifter feature was their eyes.

Taking a deep breath and pursing her lips, Priya regarded him. "What did you have in mind?"

Noting their obvious suspicion and hesitance, he shifted in the seat. Declan licked his bottom lip and imagined doing the same with sweet sugar off their bodies. "Nothing too fancy. Strawberries, Cool Whip, maybe some cupcakes."

Amani snorted half a laugh. "Cupcakes?"

He lifted a shoulder. "I thought they'd be easiest to acquire. All the good bakeries are closed this time of night."

"Then maybe we should get them in the morning." Priya purred smooth as silk.

Each syllable stroked his skin and sent delightful tingles to his cock. She leaned into him, and her sensual heat blazed against his side. While walking her fingers over his chest, sparks from her delicate tips tickled and made his dick twitch. When she paused at the final button on his shirt, she pressed her lips to the bottom of his earlobe. Oh, for the love of all that was holy, he thought he would explode from the teasing.

His eyes rolled into the back of his head. A shudder rippled through him. The dragon locked within him perked. Heaven. This had to be the Promised Land. No one would ever convince him otherwise.

"If he can survive that long," Amani sniggered. "We've been known to be a bit much for some males."

The two women, on either side of him, flicked their tongues against his neck. He shivered from the heat of their breath and their hands skimming his thighs. His skin warmed, and his cock strained within its cotton-spandex confines. The ride to their apartment needed to be shorter.

It'd be embarrassing to pop off this early. Then again, getting the first orgasm out of the way could prolong the rest of the evening's activities.

His mind danced with the potential for the evening with two feisty female felines.

Eeeeeee.

The distinct shriek tore through his skull. The beast within him jerked. His tail lashed and slammed against the mental confines holding him inside. Declan flinched, but the women seemed too busy teasing him to notice.

Not right now.

The dragon inside his mind flailed. Thrashing about and crashing into mental barriers, and he roared.

Eeeeeee.

He could miss one.

In his adult life, he answered all the other female dragons' mating summonses. Declan was under no obligation to respond to every single shriek. No one would die if he skipped out on this occasion.

Besides, two feline shifters was his fantasy. So, going to the mating grounds and rutting whatever female dragon bellowed would just be an exercise in futility. It'd never be as good as two lionesses. By him staying back, she'd have a better chance of meeting her *true* mate. Which wasn't him.

Eeeeeee. Urgency laced the cry.

His beast snapped his jaws and threw himself against Declan's mind, which kept the dragon imprisoned. Declan's human skin ran cold.

Godsdammit!

"Umm." Priya pulled back. "Is something wrong?"

Eeeeeee.

Why did it seem louder? The mating grounds were thousands of miles away. She shouldn't sound like she was right outside the car.

Somehow, Declan had missed Priya's hand on his dick. Unfortunately, instead of her finding appreciation for her and Amani's attentions, his arousal had deflated. How embarrassing.

He'd gotten to the cusp of one of his spiciest desires, and now a mating call ruined everything.

Maybe.

If he delayed answering the female dragon, another male could answer her. He just had to wait it out. If he ignored her screeching, then he could still salvage his night with the delicious women on either side of him.

Eeeeeee. He cringed as the screaming ripped through his skull.

Fuck! He had to think fast to work through this while he stalled.

"Uh." He attempted to focus on the women beside him and shut out his raging beast—not to mention the shrieking female clamoring for his attention. "Everything's fine. I'm just hungry."

Amani furrowed her brows. "You're cold. I thought dragons ran hot. Aren't you a reptile?"

Eeeeee. His dragon thrashed about inside him, demanding to be set free. Ice chilled his veins.

"I'm not a fire dragon," he forced out, trying to restrain the beast inside him.

Bringing his hand up, he pinched the bridge of his nose. For the love of the gods, he had two lionesses ready and raring to go. He and his dragon could smell their arousal. Of all the nights, why did she have to beckon him now?

"Is this like a kink thing?" Priya asked. "I mean, I guess we could stop for cupcakes."

"Oh!" Amani bounced excitedly beside him. "I've heard of this. Sploshing. It's when someone gets turned on by others sitting in cake or other foods and eating it out of them."

Priya recoiled. "Sitting in—and eating it?"

Eeeeee. The inner beast flailed. He wanted to slam his hands over his ears to stop the sound.

It wouldn't help. He'd still hear it.

"It's not that." Declan didn't mean for the words to come across so biting. His dragon had lost his ever-loving mind. "My dragon. He's throwing a fit."

Eeeeee. Another snap of the beast's jaws.

"Because you're hungry?" Priya's skepticism dripped from her words.

"I don't know about this sploshing thing. I've always been in the camp of no sugar and no dairy in my lady lion." Amani waved her hands as she set her limit.

Eeeeee. Why hadn't another dragon answered her yet? Seriously. Anyone else should have gotten there after all this time.

His dragon bellowed again, as though trying to respond. Declan shivered, and teal scales erupted as his human skin froze and flaked. Whoever that female was, she needed to shut her trap. He was busy. Eventually, *someone* else would get there and give her something to cry about.

"Oh my gods!" Priya brought her hands to her mouth. "He really *is* a dragon. I've never met a black dragon before. They're usually all white guys. But you have *scales.*"

Eeeeee.

"To be fair, he could still be a snake," Amani offered.

"No, look." Priya gripped his arm and shoved it across his chest to show her friend. "Teal! What snake do you know that's teal?"

"Holy shit." Amani's eyes widened. "A real fucking dragon."

Shaking his arm loose, he grunted. The vibe was gone. His dick had shriveled, and their pussies had dried. There'd be no way his dragon would let him have the evening he wanted. Leaning forward, clenching his teeth, he tried to swallow his beast down to prevent him from fully emerging in the car.

"Pull over," Declan demanded of their porcupine shifter Uber driver.

He had to get out of there. His dragon and whatever sow couldn't shut up had made sure to thoroughly cockblock him.

"That's probably best." Amani sighed.

Eeeeeee.

"Now," he barked, and the women on either side of him scoffed.

"You don't have to be a dick about it," Priya said.

It wasn't his intention, but it didn't matter. His beast wouldn't give him a moment's peace until he shifted and headed for the mating grounds. So help him. If he got there and some other dragon rutted her, there'd be hell to pay.

Once the driver pulled to the side of the road, Declan climbed over a yelping Priya to get out. Thankfully, Central Park was about a block away. He'd have plenty of space to shift there.

Eeeeeee.

"Bitch, I'm coming," he grumped as he took off for the open space.

3

ALISA

Perched atop one of the rugged center islands of Malin Head, Alisa's dragon screeched at the top of her lungs. Chilled sprays of salty ocean water hit her scales from the breaking waves, slamming into the northernmost tip of Ireland.

Thankfully, the seabirds of the area slept because of the hour. She hated the sound of the gulls cawing. They taunted her calls for a mate she suspected didn't exist. As usual, her throat had grown raw from the unanswered hollers. It'd be a long few days.

Unfortunately, the cloudy night prevented any views of stars or the northern lights. When her desperation went unanswered, she took solace in the beautiful evening views. Tonight, all she had to keep her company were waves and darkness.

If she had a mate, he should've come by now. Years of cycles and he hadn't shown up. This heat would be just as miserable as the previous ones.

In the past, after an unanswered heat, when she returned to her grandmother's home, she'd receive a hug and suggestions to choose a mate to end her suffering.

If only it were that easy.

Her beast wouldn't allow such a thing.

Doubts about whether any unmated dragon shifters were left crept into her thoughts. Locked inside the mind of the beast, Alisa rolled her eyes. They had a long night—and life—ahead of them if that were the case.

Again, the dragon strained her neck, opened her jaws, and bellowed loudly in yet another futile attempt to attract a male dragon to sate her ache. The more her calls went unanswered, the longer Alisa would remain imprisoned inside the dragon. Rutting was the only way out when in heat, which could last for weeks.

At this point, she'd settle for an opportunistic sheep shifter who happened past. A rut was a rut. She needed to get laid to stop the cries.

The faint smell of almonds carried on the oceanic breeze. Alisa loved almonds. Great. Now she was hungry. How long would it be until the beast would call it quits and hunt for food?

Wait.

Was that...

Trying not to get her hopes up, she turned toward the approaching sound. It could have been a weird echo from the ocean off the steep cliffs or maybe a bird flew at night.

Oooofff.

Pain rocketed through her. All the air shot out of her lungs. It had to have been a tree trunk that barreled into her gut, knocking her from her perch.

With her eyes bulging and her lungs desperate for breath, she wrapped her dragon arms around the thick shoulder that had driven into her. It took a few seconds for Alisa to gain her bearings.

They weren't falling.

Blinking and gasping, she realized it was a male that had knocked her from her spot. A teal male dragon had speared her. With his limbs wrapped around her and his sharp talons brushing against her scales, he flew them toward an open grassy area across from where she'd once been.

Finally.

What took him so long? She just wanted to get the nonsense over with so she could go back to her human life. Sometimes, especially during heat, it sucked being a female dragon shifter.

Her dragon flapped her wings, swatting them against the male.

What?

Why were they going the other direction? They were supposed to go down toward the ground and not up into the night. For the love of all that was holy, why did her dragon have to be this way?

She *wanted* this male to rut her. There was no good reason to make him fight for it. It wasn't like any other suitors were champing at the bit to get a piece of her dragon ass.

Beating her wings harder and faster, almost in an attack motion, Alisa's dragon struggled against the descent and the male who attempted to bed her.

There was nothing more annoying than instincts. Inside the mental confines of the beast's mind, Alisa pummeled her fists against the dragon.

Just get it over with. She was sure he had other human shit to do as well. They didn't need to play this stupid game. Alisa's human half despised them anyway.

The beast asked for this. Hell, she begged for it. There was absolutely no good reason to turn down this male that showed up. He was just as worthy as any.

Ignoring the human half of her existence, the dragon jammed her lower legs between herself and the male dragon. With a decent push, she could probably separate them.

But why?

She wanted to get laid. No one else answered her call. This whole earning the right to rut was absolutely absurd. Beggars couldn't be choosers. Why didn't her beast understand that?

Declan

Gorgeous. The female was absolutely stunning. Declan had never seen a golden dragon before. He wished for a break in the clouds to discover if she'd shimmer in the moonlight. She would be absolutely majestic in the sun. What he wouldn't give to witness her shine.

WHAP.

What the hell?

SLAP.

The magnificent beauty he'd just snagged for a shag battered him with her talon-tipped wings. Frantically, she flapped hard and fought their downward trajectory.

Whap. Slap. Whap. Slap.

Stunned by the sudden resistance, Declan's beast actually allowed her to gain some ground—or, well, sky. They went up instead of down.

Whap. Slap. Whap. Slap.

Not that Declan hadn't ever had to fight to rut before. Obviously, he had. Especially when others sought the same female. He'd kicked the shit out of Gideon a time or two for a sow. That was the nature of dragon sex. The male had to earn the right and conquer the female so he could have her. It was how it'd always been done.

This time felt different somehow—more urgent.

With a good thrust from her legs, she shoved him back. His hold on her nearly slipped.

Damn, she was strong. It fueled his desire for her. There was nothing more alluring, more tempting than a sow who could hold her own. His mouth watered for a chance to taste her.

Another hard kick to his gut. The force caused him to lose his grip. The pair separated. His dragon boomed his determination. He *had* to *have* her. No other options existed, and Declan had to agree. This female wouldn't defeat him. He'd rut the ever-loving shit out of her.

Besides, *she* called to *him*. This was *her* idea. He was the *only* male who had shown up. That didn't change the fact he'd give her a good battle. She wanted it rough. He could make it downright nasty.

Pumping his wings, Declan's dragon chased her. He wasn't about to be bested by a female. The rumble shook his chest before it exploded in a loud roar. The golden sow didn't seem to even notice. She kept going farther over the ocean.

If she thought she could interrupt his night with the lionesses and then just fly away, she had another thing coming. He'd play the game. His dragon had a good thousand or so pounds on the female. It wouldn't take much to get her to submit.

With his heart racing, he beat his wings harder, flying faster.

Just a little more.

Finally, he caught up. Soaring a few feet above her, he counted the steady beat of her flapping wings. If he timed it just right, he could drop on top of her and essentially ride her back to land. There'd be no way she could sustain flight with his added bulk.

They hadn't gotten too far out, so it'd be pretty easy. The excitement of the chase surged through him and made his dragon dick pulse with want.

Five. Six. Seven and eight!

On the last count, Declan's dragon dropped, and his full bulk collided with the golden beauty. The thrill of the hunt coursed through his veins, swirling in his balls. There was nothing more exciting than battling for the right to rut a female.

Gotcha!

She let out an ear-piercing howl as he wrapped his legs around her. It wasn't a mating call. No, she'd bellowed a cry of frustration. It tickled Declan's growing desire.

The sudden added weight made her wobble, but she kept going. What a determined little wench. His heart fluttered, and he admired her perseverance. The need to have her consumed his every motivation.

He would win this battle.

She would submit to him, and they would rut.

Never had his beast been so determined to lie with a female.

Sliding his talons along her shoulders, he sought a seam in her scales. He wanted to get a good grip on her. When she jerked to the left abruptly, in what he assumed was an attempt to buck him off, he held on tighter. She couldn't knock him loose that easily.

Aha!

Jabbing his dragon claws in, the tips of his talons pierced into her soft flesh. She bellowed a pain-filled screech and dipped down. The sound rattled through his bones and made his cock and balls vibrate.

He never wanted a female as much as he needed this one. Not even the pair of lionesses compared to his desperation for this sow.

His grip was too secure. She couldn't shake him without seriously injuring herself.

Check and mate.

With a jerk of his arms, he sliced through her skin beneath her scales. This move allowed him to wrap his fingers around the muscles. He controlled her wings. She couldn't flap anymore. He had to do the flying in order for them not to plummet down into the ocean.

4

ALISA

Lightning bolts flashed across Alisa's vision. Blinding pain tore through her shoulders where her wings met her back.

What the hell?

That fucker jammed his godsdamn claws into her! Others just scratched. This was excessive.

Now, he actively prevented her from flapping her wings.

What an asshole.

Even with advanced shifter healing, it'd take at least an hour, if not more, to recover from an injury like that. Such a dick move.

Whipping her tail left and right, she did all she could to control how they flew. It might have started out as her dragon following instincts, but he made it personal. There was no reason he had to tear into her like that. She'd be damned if he got to rut her without a fight now.

Her human anger tangled with her dragon's arousal. The beast inside her craved a male who could take what he wanted. This was the exact outcome she desired when she went into heat. At times Alisa's humanness disagreed with the feral nature of her dragon.

He'd turned them around and ascended higher into the night sky. When he'd dropped his big ass onto her, she'd lost altitude.

They hadn't quite skimmed the cresting waves, but they'd gotten close. Half of her had hoped they would've splashed into the ocean, if for no other reason than to knock him off.

Unfortunately, he was in control, so she had to come up with a different plan if she wanted to escape what would, no doubt, be a violent rutting.

Her stomach and her pussy betrayed her. They fluttered at the mere thought of being fucked roughly by this male.

Ugh! Stupid beast.

Arching her back only made his grip pierce deeper. The razor blade-like talons of his fingers severed the fibers of her muscles. The pain was somewhat tolerable. It wasn't quite a dull ache, but it no longer blurred her vision.

They closed in on the grass-covered stones. There wasn't much soil beneath those green blades. The teal dragon flying on her back did little to cushion the landing.

She swore internally as he pressed his head down onto her so her chin would be the first to meet the mountain.

WHAM.

They slammed into the ground. Squeezing her eyes shut, fireworks flashed behind her lids as a new pain ripped through her. Bikers got road rash when they slid along the asphalt. Alisa got mountain rash.

Scales flew off, and her flesh tore along the jagged stones. The coppery smell of her own blood filled the air. She wouldn't be surprised if their impact left a skid mark of her blood along the mountaintop. The taste danced on her tongue.

As he slowed his wings, dirt and moss got stuck between her teeth. Together, they slid to a stop.

Shit. Was that a stone, or did she lose a tooth?

What a fucking dick.

Speaking of which. Ever since he plopped his fat ass on her back, his throbbing, nubbed dragon erection pressed against her spine. As with most dragons, the chase or the battle turned him on.

Unfortunately, her dragon was raring to go as well.

Despite the immense pain thundering throughout her body, her scales were heated for him. Magma surged through her, and her core pulsed in greedy need. To add insult to injury, her human consciousness succumbed to the hedonism coursing through her veins.

Just another reason to hate her dragon instincts. In nonanimal form, she wasn't one of those people who craved to be tossed around like a rag doll. However, as a beast, she couldn't get enough.

The rougher, the better. Spilling blood was her beast's aphrodisiac. Her dragon wanted to be taken and claimed. When she was in heat, the toxic pheromones and hormones made Alisa's human half surrender to dominant male displays. Her sex throbbed with desire. She'd never been this slick before.

To make matters worse, he let out the loudest, most triumphant roar just above her head. Her ears rang as she blinked and shook to stop it.

Who the hell was he yelling to anyway? No one else answered the call. So, he didn't have to proclaim his conquest like some dumbass. So far, she was pretty sure she'd hate this dragon in any other circumstance, but at the mating grounds, this did it for her.

Nothing was more infuriating.

Despite Alisa's annoyance with his unnecessary victory cry, Alisa's dragon shuddered. Her body craved this male. Deep in the throes of her heat, nothing would satisfy her but this male rutting her.

Fire sliced through her shoulder as he removed his talons from the wounds. Her core blazed hotter. The pain was like a lightning bolt to her clit. Her beast swooned at this type of foreplay. Her animal half arched her back, swiped her tail aside, and offered herself to the teal male dragon.

Shivering in greedy submissive need beneath him, she crooned a moan as the chill of his breath graced her neck. When he sniffed, scenting her, she swallowed hard.

Delightful agony stole the breath from her lungs when his long dragon teeth clamped on her. She thrashed in passion beneath him as jaws closed tighter.

He. Fucking. Bit. Her!

As dual beings residing in the same existence, Alisa couldn't help but be consumed by the effects of her beast's arousal. While relegated to the confines of their mind at the moment, the need the dragon had pulsed through her human half as well. It banished any and all rational thought. The only thing that mattered was sating her heat.

She had to have his dragon cock *now*.

After the male swiped his tongue along the bite mark on her shoulder, he readjusted himself. The anticipation of what was to come made her dizzy. She craved the feel of him. Her pussy quivered, eager to be further claimed.

Curling her talon-tipped dragon claws into the grass beneath her, she took a deep breath in expectation of the inevitable. She and her beast were in sync. This was the only thing either of them wanted.

When he slammed his thick dragon dick inside her, every nubbin lining his shaft stimulated all her sensitive spots. She couldn't help but groan as the ecstasy washed over her. There was no better sex than dragon sex.

Each of his aggressive thrusts into her slick pussy begged her human form to come forward. Teal scales rained around her, meaning he shifted back as well. His body would turn human, but his cock would remain dragon—thick, tapered, and blessed with a thousand buds of stimulation.

The exquisite pain of a transition during mating only enhanced the experience. Her golden scales joined the growing pile as her muzzle shrunk to a human face. Each nub on his dick shocked her core. Her bones cracked as her arms and legs reshaped into human limbs, making her scream in both pleasure and agony. Every time he withdrew, she ached to be filled again. When he slammed home, she discovered ecstasy.

Fingers dug into her soft hips as he dragged her back onto his thick cock. She shuddered at the fullness of his dick stretching her pussy. With her vision blurring, she quaked in bliss.

Her dark hair hung down as she bounced back and forth with each one of his claiming plunges. She fast approached release, and her muscles tightened. Every cell of her body was on fire, craving more—harder, faster, deeper. She needed everything, the pain and the ecstasy he offered.

Panting, she couldn't catch her breath in the face of his vigor. He fucked her with a vengeance. Alisa and her dragon couldn't get enough, rolling her hips and sensually howling in the night's darkness.

When his hands slid down over her hips toward her sex, she gasped. His thick fingers assaulted her clit, and her knees gave out. Thankfully, he not only held her up, preventing her from crashing against the ground again, but he rolled them. Their bodies were joined. His cock was deep inside her, pummeling her pussy into submission as she now sat atop him.

The change in angle drove the head of his dragon cock up against her G-spot, and she screamed. Leaning forward, she rested her hands on his shins as she convulsed. It'd been a long time since she'd fucked in reverse cowgirl, and she *never* did it at the mating grounds. This was a uniquely human position.

Pulling her downward, he slammed up inside her before she could get her bearings. Everything exploded. Her nerves vibrated. Her pussy was on fire. She dug her nails into his flesh as her orgasm ripped through her.

5

DECLAN

Holy fucking hell. Her cunt gripped Declan's cock like a vise. As she circled her hips, her walls spasmed, and he swore he left this plane of existence.

So godsdamn snug.

His balls tightened, and he arched his back. Would she erupt again? Could he shove her over a second orgasmic cliff before she milked his release?

Running his hand up her spine, he slid his fingers in her sweat and the blood dripping from the deep but healing wounds he'd created. She shivered when he reached the base of her neck, and she bucked on his dick.

Delicious female. He could still taste her blood on his lips from when his dragon had bitten her. How he craved to know if her pussy was just as sweet.

Another time.

His fingers entangled in her long dark strands. Taking hold of them, he fisted her hair and tugged, jerking her head backward and threw her off-balance. The possessive growl rumbled in his chest as he thrust deeper inside her. His dragon wanted to *own* her—*claim* her. Make the golden female *his*.

He loved things that glittered, and nothing shimmered like a golden dragon.

With her head yanked back at an impossible angle, he sat up so his chest met her slick back. Blood stained her healing cheek, which had only been briefly marred from the collision with the ground. Turning her head slightly, he had access to her open mouth if he wanted it. But more importantly, he could see the lust in her eyes—the feral, hedonistic greed. The blood and dirt staining her visage didn't deter him. He considered it a sign of his triumph over her.

Her bruised and slightly battered features were kind of hot.

His cock twitched, buried so far inside her that he swore he could feel her kidneys.

"Blood looks good on you," he thundered. They weren't his words. The dragon found a way to speak through him.

Not only had the beast stolen control of his vocal cords, but his dragon opened his jaw. Declan dipped his head and bit down hard on her shoulder again.

While he didn't have the sharp canines of his dragon maw, he still had the power of the beast. Effortlessly, he broke skin. The copper flavor spilled onto his tongue. She screamed and jerked against him.

She was his now.

As her sex clamped down on him tighter than before, he jammed his cock deeper and erupted inside her. The roar of his orgasm was stifled by her shoulder in his mouth.

Wrapping his arms around her, he held her tight against him as he rode the wave of pleasure and lashed his tongue through the blood oozing into his mouth. Still clenching his ass, he continued to push himself inside her but with much less enthusiasm.

Once he released her shoulder, he turned his head and swiped his tongue along his lower lip. Warm, moist blood and sweat greeted his cheek when he pressed it to her back. Closing his eyes, he tried to catch his own breath. He listened to the thundering beat of the golden dragon's heart. The rhythm matched his own.

Two became one.

Gasping, she leaned against him as he gently lay down. Once his body met the ground, Declan let his arms slide from around her. Balanced atop him, her legs splayed, she panted.

The last portion of his shift occurred as his dick slid from inside her. It morphed to human proportions. With a sigh, his dragon curled into a ball within the recesses of his mind. The beast was content with their rutting.

"Did." She gulped air. "Did you bite me?"

Reflexively, he chuckled. "Yeah, that's sort of part of this."

"Are you serious?" She scrambled over him.

Her movements tickled, and his laughter grew.

Standing over him, she ran her hand over her shoulder. "Dick!" she hissed.

Resting on his elbows, Declan sat up slightly. The humor gone, he peered at her. "*You* called *me* here. These are the mating grounds. What did you expect? It's supposed to get rough."

Slapping her hands over her healing face, she scrubbed. The mountain rash slowly evaporated from her visage, but the grime remained. After she let out a rumbled cry of frustration, she uncovered her features. Popping her fists on her hips, she glared at him.

"You didn't have to do *that*!"

"Your dragon loved it."

"Asshole," she snarled.

In the moon's glow, he drank her in. Though mussed, her wavy deep-brown hair fell past her shoulders. Her flushed features were rounded yet familiar—he must have seen her somewhere before. Even with his advanced shifter vision, he couldn't tell the color of her eyes. All he knew was that they were dark.

He allowed his gaze to drift lower, and his cock stirred at the sight of large breasts. They weren't perky. Their weight wouldn't allow for that, but his mouth watered at the prospect of pawing them and sucking on her still stiff nipples.

There was a crease in her soft belly. His fingers tingled, wanting to take hold of her again for another round. Thick thighs were met with a tuft of dark curls at the apex.

She was the most magnificent woman he'd ever seen. Now that he'd had a taste of her, he wanted more. Swallowing the last hint of the flavor of her blood, he studied her.

She raked her hands through her hair while letting out a heavy breath. Almost as though she were nervous, she crossed her arms and winced. "Fuck."

"What's wrong?" he asked as he sat up farther before getting to his own feet.

The question earned him yet another sideways glare. "Are you joking?"

It dawned on him, and he lifted his brows. "Oh."

When his dragon robbed her of the ability to fly, he'd done some serious damage. It would take a few hours for her to heal from those wounds.

Remorse nestled in his gut. He'd never meant to harm her. The beast just got amorous. "Sorry." He scrubbed the back of his neck.

She wouldn't make eye contact with him as she rotated her shoulders.

Dammit.

The guilt ball in his stomach doubled in size. He'd really hurt her.

That hadn't been his intention. He'd never had someone fight him so hard before. All he did was match energy. It wasn't his fault it went as far as it did. If she didn't want an injury, she shouldn't have struggled so ferociously.

Okay, that was a dick thought. He had to do something to make it better.

"Do you want a massage?" he offered, unsure what else to say.

She scoffed. "It'll heal. Why are you not addressing the bigger problem?"

Blinking, he racked his brain for whatever she meant.

From where he stood, they'd done the standard dragon thing. They fought for dominance. They got bloody. He won. They rutted. What the hell was she talking about?

Oh. Right. "The bite?"

Emphatically, her eyes widened, and she nodded. "Yeah. That's kind of a big deal."

This he felt confident in.

With a smile, he waved a hand as though this would dismiss her concerns. "You didn't bite me back. We can't be mates unless you mark me, too."

His dragon huffed. What was that about?

"Seriously. Nothing to get excited about. I'm just passionate."

"Oh my gods. You're an idiot," she groaned, rolling her eyes.

Annoyance flared in his chest as his dragon lazily thumped his tail up and down. "You're making a mountain out of a molehill. You called me to the mating grounds. We rutted. And now we go on with our lives." A possibility occurred to him. "Is this your first time here?"

Maybe she'd recently drunk the releaser elixir. Female dragons could prevent being plagued by their heat if they consumed a potion made by the Ember Witches. Any dragon with means took that opportunity. It was only when they were ready for mating that they returned to the witches to get their heat. It was possible she hadn't experienced this before.

He wasn't necessarily assuming her to be a virgin. Dragon females could bed plenty without going into heat. Again, his dragon huffed. Apparently, he didn't like the idea of the golden dragon with others. Either way, he had to consider this was her inaugural visit to the mating grounds, looking for a mate.

That would explain how hard she fought. Plus, he had to admit he'd been rougher than he'd been in the past. Not that she knew that. If she'd never been through a heat cycle, she would never have had a dragon answer her call. Obviously, he'd taken her dragon cherry.

Pride welled in his chest. His dragon preened within his mind.

Since she didn't understand how things went, he figured he should explain it. "Blood is always spilled when my dragon or I fuck. Not to sound conceited or anything, it's just how it is for us, but I've been to the mating grounds a ton."

Unfortunately, male dragons didn't have a way to stop hearing the mating call of a female dragon in heat. They were slaves to it. By nature, an adult male of his age heard dozens of beckonings. Though, if she had never been before, he probably shouldn't bring that up.

"Anyway. If my bites meant anything, I would've had a mate by now. I wouldn't have heard your call. Mutual markings equal mating. We didn't do that. So, we are not. You're free and clear."

Confident he'd eased her concerns, he grinned.

She stared blankly at him.

Maybe she still processed his words. It was a lot to digest. He'd give her a minute to catch up. It was a lot for a female dragon to come to the mating grounds for the first time. He probably should have been gentler.

That guilt ball returned.

Shaking her head, she pivoted on her heel and walked toward the mainland, putting distance between them and the crashing ocean beneath them.

What was her problem?

"Where are you going?" he asked as he jogged to catch up.

"Away from you."

Declan stopped. There was no winning with this female. Watching her stomp, his dragon urged him to follow, but the human half didn't move. She didn't want him around. He wasn't about to chase the woman.

The beast inside him rumbled his displeasure in his mind.

Too bad. The dragon needed to understand. She was quite clear—she'd gotten what she came for from him. His presence was neither desired nor required.

She made her preferences known. He prided himself on listening to what women told him. If she wanted space, he wouldn't go after her. She'd be alright. Eventually, she'd heal.

Turning his back on her, Declan summoned his dragon to take flight.

6

ALISA

Three hours.

It'd taken three godsdamned hours for what he did to heal. Thankfully, Alisa found a herd of sheep and nestled against one of them for a brief nap while waiting for her back to mend. The stupid teal dragon had practically destroyed her shoulder muscles. Resting with farm animals was all she could think to do until she could fly again. However, since she waited, the flight to Manhattan was mostly pain-free.

In all the years she'd endured her heat, *never* had a male been *so* violent. Or skilled at rutting. But that didn't matter. He'd bitten her. None of the others had *ever* bitten her. He had a lot of fucking nerve sinking his teeth into her.

Recalling how he sliced into her skin made her shudder as a wave of warmth washed over her. Her core pulsed, and her nipples tightened.

Fuck, that was a good rut.

But she couldn't focus on that. He'd committed the most egregious of sins. She expected talons. They were inevitable. Dragons were not gentle lovers, and that was the best part of bedding dragon males. Bumps and bruises were the nature of things.

But a bite? Hell no.

That was a commitment she hadn't signed up for.

From what she knew about mating, biting meant the bond was initiated.

Asshole.

The only way to solidify it would be for her to mark him in return. She had no intention of doing that. Hell would have to freeze over first.

He was a dick. Albeit a talented and attractive dick, but a dick nonetheless. So, she'd just have to ride out this half bond until it fizzled. Hopefully, it wouldn't take long considering her human half already thought he was a giant tool bag.

Besides, if they didn't see each other again, there shouldn't be any concern. He wouldn't be able to trigger the yearning mates had for one another. Avoidance was the best way to endure the inevitable tumultuous experience of a half bond.

What a jackass. She hoped his suffering was worse, considering he started this mess. It would teach him a lesson about biting unwilling females. And he had the nerve to say it was a habit of his. What kind of idiot did such irresponsible things?

Her dragon snarled at the thought of the others being bitten by him.

She rolled her eyes at her inner beast. That creature was a lost cause.

In the early morning hours, the sun broke on the horizon. Alisa landed on the roof of the apartment building from which she had left. She endured a thousand and one inconveniences for being a female dragon at the mercy of her heat, but the absolute worst had to be the forced shifts.

Clothing didn't morph with her. So, she either ripped her clothes to shreds because it came on so quickly or she had to remember where she took off. It was the only way she could come back and collect her garments.

She couldn't just abandon outfits whenever her dragon got horny. That'd get expensive real quick. While she did okay as a bartender, New York City was not exactly a cheap place to live.

Thankfully, this heat hadn't come on as intensely as some previous ones. It awarded her the time to make a mental note of where she'd left her stuff. She wouldn't have to scurry through her apartment building nude, trying to avoid her neighbors. There were only so many excuses for a naked woman running through the halls.

Humans didn't know about shifters. She'd be damned if she was the one to let them in on the secret. The Council of Others, the governing body of all things nonhuman, had strict rules and horrendous consequences for those who exposed supernatural beings. The threat of them was enough for Alisa to keep her existence hush-hush. Considering she was already shunned in one way, she didn't need to make it worse by outing herself.

Thankfully, a woman strolling down the hall wearing wrinkled clothes from the previous day with her head down was socially acceptable. The walk of shame was universal and didn't solicit questions. People made their assumptions, and Alisa was content with her reputation taking a hit, as opposed to her well-being. What did she care if humans she'd never see again thought her promiscuous?

Shifters didn't worry about such human assumptions. Rutting was natural. She didn't pay attention to who knew when she fucked someone.

Thoroughly dressed, with her coffee from the best bodega on the block in hand and a bag full of Plan B, she paused at the door to her building. Four morning-after pills might be overkill, but she wasn't taking any chances. A baby dragon was not on her agenda. Since she didn't have the magic birth control elixir from the Ember Witches, she had to do the next best thing—human measures to prevent pregnancy.

"Good morning." A smooth, unfamiliar male voice startled her.

Turning sharply to face the source, she held her apartment key between her fingers as though it would be some sort of defense. A woman couldn't be too careful.

Her jaw dropped. How had he found her?

"H-uh-hi," she stammered.

Standing at the curb in a charcoal suit with his hands clasped before him was Duncan Hayes—her father. A barrage of questions ricocheted through her mind. This couldn't have happened at a worse time. She wasn't ready. This wasn't how she wanted to meet her father—with the scent of a male dragon on her and fresh from the mating grounds.

"I'm sorry we didn't get to speak yesterday."

Blinking, she froze, unable to move. Her heart hammered, but words wouldn't cross her lips.

He'd been aware she was there the day before.

"Had I known you were coming, I would've blocked out my morning."

Just the morning? That didn't seem like enough time to discuss anything. Resentment coiled around her ribs. She deserved more than just a few hours at the start of the business day. She *was* his daughter, after all.

"I was hoping you had an hour or so today."

"Um," she uttered, unsure how to respond. She absolutely wanted to talk to him, but she wasn't prepared.

Over the years, she'd imagined this moment. Every time the conversation went differently. In some of her made-up scenarios, it'd been contentious while others were filled with affection and apologies. However, not one of them started with him approaching her. She'd always been the one to make first contact. It gave her the control over how the discussion went. By him showing up at her apartment unannounced, the ball was in his court. She hadn't planned for that.

"No pressure." He held his hands up, palms out, as though to show he wasn't a threat.

That was easy for him to say. He wasn't the one who'd just gone into heat and had a gut full of dragon swimmers while meeting his father for the first time. That situation needed to be taken care of sooner rather than later. She wasn't ready to be a single mother. It hadn't gone so well for her mom.

The stress of the last few hours made her head throb.

"I thought, since you showed up at my office, you wanted to talk." Genuine kindness and sincerity filled his words.

Unable to make her voice work, Alisa nodded slowly.

To be fair, the desire to speak with him nagged at her every day of her life. She yearned to learn about what had happened to her mother. All she knew was that it had to do with him.

"You don't have to invite me inside." He glanced down the street momentarily. "I believe there is a coffee shop not too far from here—maybe a block away."

He was right. There was a pretentious café with bougie flavored caffeine drinks close by. She'd never actually *drunk* anything from there. The prices were astronomical for a mere beverage, but she smelled it from her apartment every morning, and the scent was divine.

If only she could get it together and actually formulate multisyllable words.

"Okay," she said. "Sure." Close enough.

He smiled, and the warmth in his expression washed over her. One foot in front of the other, she descended the stairs toward her father. Her heart lodged in her throat as a myriad of emotions swirled in her chest.

She'd anticipated this moment forever. Anxiety had her fingers tightening around the bag of pregnancy prevention. Excitement for the potential relationship with the man who'd contributed to half her existence had her heart thundering in her ears as she joined him on the sidewalk. They walked side by side to get overpriced coffee and talk.

7

DECLAN

Ever since Declan's best friend, Gideon, had mated several months ago, Declan didn't see him often. The same company employed them, but they were in different departments. Gideon designed some of the most beautiful jewelry Declan had ever seen. Declan's role within Arach Jewelry had to do with brand and content marketing. He worked from home most of the time.

He and Gideon hadn't hung out that often before—maybe once or twice a week. They were dragon males, after all. Dragons weren't pack creatures. The males tended to be loners until they took mates. So, it made sense Gideon had backed off, but Declan missed the opportunity to discuss things his acquaintances wouldn't understand.

Sure, he had shifter friends. They understood a bulk of his life experience, but being a dragon had its own nuances that other beings couldn't even fathom. The scarcity of his kind across the world meant meeting others outside of the mating grounds a rarity. So, having a confidant in his own city had made life easier.

Not that Declan resented the mating—not entirely anyway. Maybe he was jealous. It had to be nice having a connection.

Nah.

That couldn't be it. He networked with shifters every time he went out. He missed his wingman. That was all. Being out on the prowl was far less creepy when done in pairs. Going it alone was kind of cringe.

Either way, it'd be good to see his friend again early this morning. He really needed the company of another dragon.

Giving his shoulders a good shake, he exited the gym locker room and headed to the suspended track to get a warm-up run in. At that hour, almost no one was up there. Most, especially humans, opted for the treadmills. Declan preferred real running as opposed to machines. It allowed him to zone out—almost meditate with no other distractions around. Jogging was his thinking time. Or, when Gideon showed up, he had the opportunity to chat with his good friend.

Once at the entrance of the running area, he stood off to the side. Bending his right leg, he pulled his ankle against the back of his thigh, giving his muscles a decent stretch while scanning the few runners for his buddy. Everyone who chose the track that morning was a shifter of some kind. Gideon had texted that he'd arrived a few minutes ahead of him.

There he was, rounding the far curve and headed toward Declan. Dropping his foot, he lifted the other and did the same move before Gideon passed.

"Hey," Declan greeted, lifting his chin as he jogged to his friend's side.

"What's up?" Gideon asked.

"Oh man," Declan hung his head. "Have you ever been in the perfect situation and then a call interrupts it?"

No other shifters dealt with mating beckonings that he knew of. This was uniquely a dragon struggle. He couldn't talk about it with anyone else. Only Gideon understood.

Snorting, Gideon grinned. "Of course."

"I had these beautiful lionesses." Declan shook his head, recalling how the previous evening had started.

"Lionesses?" Gideon repeated. "As in more than one?"

"Yeah!" Declan puffed his chest slightly as the two of them continued to jog. His dragon grumbled internally.

What the hell?

Normally, he relished sharing his conquests.

His friend chuckled. "Isn't that like your dream scenario?"

"Absolutely. Lionesses, cougars, leopards, tigers—I adore anyone feline."

"But you were summoned? And went?"

The confidence and pride deflated from Declan's chest. "Yeah."

His dragon snorted in his mind.

"Why didn't you just ignore it?"

"I tried!"

Gideon's brows rose.

"She just got louder and louder in my head."

"Was she close or something?"

"No." Declan shook his head. "She was at the grounds."

"Hmm." Gideon half shrugged. "The volume never increased for me. I could tune them out if I was busy."

Declan furrowed his brows and frowned. He'd had the same experience. Anytime he'd tried to ignore a call in favor of something else, he could. To be fair, he hadn't done it all that often. He actually enjoyed rutting dragons. Most of the time, it hadn't been inconvenient for him.

"You think it's 'cause you're ice and I'm fire?" Gideon never missed an opportunity to gloat about being a fire dragon. They were supposedly the most powerful of all the shifters. As an ice dragon, according to lore, Declan wasn't *as* enchanted. Though, he'd never quite understood what that meant. Who measured that sort of thing? He was pretty sure if he went toe to toe with Gideon, he'd kick his ass. He wouldn't even need his ice.

Rolling his eyes, he playfully punched Gideon in the shoulder. It only made his friend laugh harder. "That wasn't even the weirdest thing."

"Yeah?"

"After—" Declan wouldn't get too into the weeds on this part. He didn't need to give Gideon the graphic play-by-play. He knew what happened at the mating grounds. "She was *pissed*."

"Why?" Gideon asked. "Couldn't find the little man in the canoe?"

His friend's chiding grated against Declan's nerves. His dragon harrumphed within his mind, also unamused. Here he tried to talk about something serious, and all his friend had were jokes.

Gideon continued. "It only happened once, but I pissed off a female in that situation. It was after I met Ella. Not only had I gone deaf to the call, but I couldn't complete the deed."

"Really?" Declan had a vague memory of that. His friend had practically been a raving lunatic when he first mated with Ella. He was all out of sorts and filled with denial.

"It was awful," Gideon lamented. "I went there and waited for a sow 'cause, you remember, I wasn't hearing any summonses. This female showed up, and I gave it everything

I had. I got her to the ground and then *nothing*. She was furious. Which she had every right to be. I had no business being there wasting her time."

Several months ago, his friend had accidentally mated with a human woman. He'd gone deaf to the mating calls of female dragons. Which, in retrospect, made sense, considering he was bonded. He didn't have a reason to answer anyone else's beckoning. His mate just happened to be a human. It'd been quite the ordeal, but in the end, they got the blessing from the Council of Others, and from the looks of it, he was pretty happy.

"So, why was she mad at you?" The mirth in Gideon's tone taunted Declan. He didn't have to be so smug. "Didn't you get her to the finish line?"

"Are you fucking kidding me?" Declan scoffed. "Of course I did. I'm very capable when it matters."

Gideon continued to chuckle.

Declan's inner beast rumbled softly in his mind. His annoyance with their friend grew.

"It was the most intense battle to rut I've ever had."

"Nice."

"Blood everywhere."

"She get you?"

Shaking his head, Declan puffed his chest in pride. "Nah. All hers."

Gideon nodded.

"I don't know about you, but when I'm at the mating grounds, it's not a soft, gentle affair."

Gideon snorted. "Is it for anyone?"

Declan shrugged. "Anyway, so I'm really into it. Right? And I bit her—"

"Wait." His friend held up a hand and slowed his jogging to a stop.

Declan paused. "You okay? Got a cramp or something?"

"You *bit* a female dragon *at the mating grounds*?"

He regarded Gideon curiously. "Yeah?" Was that something his friend didn't normally do? "So?"

Gideon blinked furiously. "You *bit* her?"

"She didn't return it. So, it's not like we're mated or anything." Why was he making such a big deal out of this?

"Dude."

"I've bitten sows before."

"Why?"

Again, Declan shrugged. "I go where the mood takes me."

Gideon arched a brow. "That's a cavalier attitude to have toward mating. I'd be pissed too if some random asshole went around marking everyone he came across."

"That's not what I'm doing. It's not that serious. I'm just passionate."

"Call it whatever you want, but you claimed that female."

"Whatever." Declan shook his head as though to dismiss his friend's insinuation. "It's moot. She didn't mark me back. We didn't mate."

"Yeah. I wouldn't be so confident if I were you. Ella didn't bite me, but she scratched me and that was enough. It could've been the littlest nick. You just might be mated."

"I think I'd know if I was marked and thus *mated*."

The grin spreading on Gideon's face was laced with smugness. "Okay. If you say so."

Declan did.

Lifting his head, he jogged again. His friend was a pace behind. What did Gideon know about dragon mating anyway? He'd mated with a human. All he had was speculation and the shit they were taught as kids. Declan was living the dragon life. He'd recognize if he mated the sow. There would be some sort of pull or emotion if they'd created a bond. He hadn't felt a damn thing. So, as he had told the female, they hadn't mutually marked, and he'd done it before. There was nothing to worry about.

The dragon snorted inside his mind again. He could shut his face too. He was just an animal and acted on instincts. This was far more complicated than that. Besides, the beast had done all the biting. If there was any drama because of it, it would totally be Declan's dragon's fault, not Declan's.

Another beastly snort.

Whatever.

8

ALISA

Out of necessity, Alisa had ditched her bodega beverage while they walked. It seemed like a bad idea to go out for coffee with one in her hand. However, now that she sat with the fancy macchiato in front of her, caffeine was the last thing she wanted. A stiff drink would be better.

At least she'd excused herself to take the pills in the bathroom. With one problem solved, she faced the other.

Sitting across from her, at a small table near the window, was Duncan Hayes. The man she'd wondered about her entire life. The guy her mother spent sleepless nights weeping over and the reason she'd died, according to her grandmother.

Over the whooshing of the coffee machines and the soft jazz music, they'd had a pleasant enough conversation thus far, albeit superficial. It had all the earmarks of a job interview.

He'd shared how he'd moved to Manhattan years ago to grow his business. She'd answered his questions about school and work. They hadn't gotten into the meat and potatoes of anything.

That was until he asked, "What brought you to Manhattan?"

She'd already explained she'd only moved there recently and had been raised upstate, in the mountains. Most dragons preferred open spaces to tight cities. She stared at the foam in the oversized mug. Should she be honest? That felt far too forward and blunt for the style of conversation they'd had thus far. Would he believe her if she lied? Fibbing wouldn't do any good. She came for answers. Now was as good a time as any to try for them.

"You." She went with the truth and met his gaze to study his reaction. "My mom never spoke much about you before she died."

He winced slightly.

"And after, my grandmother, who raised me, said you weren't something I should be concerned about. Eventually, I wore her down. She told me your name, but that was it. You were easy enough to find."

Glancing away, she fidgeted with her fingers. "My mom had an old picture of the two of you. So, when I googled your name, you looked like the guy in the photo." Licking her bottom lip, she met his gaze. "I figured it had to be you."

He cleared his throat and brought his espresso to his lips, taking a slow sip. Turning his attention to the window, he got a faraway look in his eye. "I see."

Nothing else. He just stared.

Pressing her lips together, she attempted patience. A thousand and one questions bounced in her brain, but she wanted him to be the one to speak.

The silence between them hung heavily on Alisa's shoulders.

Why didn't he talk? There was definitely more to the story.

She couldn't sit there listening to the jazz music. She had to fill the void.

"I don't *want* anything from you. I don't need your money." She leaned forward as the words tumbled from her mouth. "Can I get to know you?" And what happened to her mother and between them? Her grandmother had been vague about everything, and Alisa wasn't there when she died.

With a furrowed brow, he returned his focus to her. Pursing his lips, he lowered his cup to the saucer. Until that moment, he'd been relaxed and friendly. Now his expression seemed to carry pain.

Did he regret what he'd done—leaving her mother and Alisa for someone else?

Her mother spent countless nights of Alisa's youth sobbing and asking the fates why they had stolen her mate. Her agony had been palpable.

"I'm sorry I never met you before this," he admitted in a tone laced with guilt. "I should have, at the very least, been involved with some of your milestones."

"So, you were aware of me?" She'd always thought he hadn't been informed.

He let out a heavy sigh. "Yes. I was there when you were laid."

A spear pierced her old childhood wound.

Once fertilized, a female dragon carried an egg for six weeks. They didn't have live births. Instead, they birthed an egg, which must be warmed and tended to for another six weeks before it hatched into a baby dragon.

Her father knew she existed. He'd witnessed her being lain. The revelation ripped her heart to shreds. He walked away after seeing her egg. As far as she was concerned, no sin was greater than abandoning a hatchling.

Having grown up without him, she almost hoped her mother and grandmother had lied and never actually told him she existed. Instead, he knew of her and still ignored her.

That knowledge somehow made her pain worse.

Swallowing it down, she tried to focus on the how. It made little sense. Why would he go to another female if he had one and a child on the way?

Until that point, he seemed like a logical man. Their conversation had flowed nicely, and she understood how he'd gotten his success. But leaving her mother in that situation—what reason could he have to abandon them?

Had she—had her mother—misunderstood the relationship? "You were with my mother for years, weren't you? Like you were together."

"Yes." He nodded as he used the tips of his fingers to turn his cup. "We'd grown up together. And as adults, we were involved with one another for a long time, but we never officially bonded."

"Why not?" She hadn't meant to sound incredulous, but the words just slipped out. It was almost like she'd inherited her mother's feelings of loss and betrayal.

So many dragons she'd known settled for a partner outside their species. Considering their own kind were rare, finding your true dragon mate—that was essentially a fairy tale. That never happened anymore. It didn't matter how many trips to the mating grounds a female took, the one fate chose for her could have selected another or died in battle for her. No one was guaranteed a dragon mate.

He tightened his lips and again gazed out the window. "We weren't true. Fate hadn't tied our futures."

"Did you even try?"

He snapped his attention back to her. "Many times."

Sitting back, she regarded him with suspicion.

"We marked each other every chance we got, but it wasn't enough," he said before taking a gulp of his espresso. "I'd just started Arach. The beginning years were extremely difficult. I was open to choosing Vivienne and forsaking my true mate. She only had to wait. It isn't a quick process. You can't rush a chosen mate. I did everything I could. Back then, I would have done anything to have her be my true destined mate, but she just wasn't. Fate had other plans. I'm only a male. I cannot ignore the calls of *all* female dragons. Especially, the beckoning of my true mate. Fate doesn't allow for that. There wasn't anything I could do as an unmated male."

Alisa didn't understand. They'd marked each other. That was what created the bond. How could they not be mated if they'd each shed one another's blood—and on multiple occasions, apparently?

It reminded her of the teal dragon. Her hand went to her shoulder reflexively. Maybe he was right. If fate didn't bless their union, they weren't mated. At least, according to her father, that was what had happened between her parents.

Dropping her hand, she blinked, trying to process all she'd been told before and presently. It was far too perplexing to sort through and make sense of in that moment.

"I wasn't in a place to start a family." Duncan Hayes's words broke into her thoughts and drew her attention. "I wanted our mating to be solid before we ever brought an egg into it." He leaned over the table and reached for her hands. "Vivienne got impatient. She took the fertility potion without my knowledge."

"So, that's why you left her?" Alisa asked as she pulled her hands out of his.

"No." The agony in his eyes magnified.

She expected to see anger, but there was only pain.

If she were in his shoes, she'd be pissed as hell if someone tried to trap her with a pregnancy. Her hand went to her stomach. Those four morning-after doses better do their damn job. She wanted no part of single motherhood. It had destroyed her mom.

Taking another deep breath, her father shifted his gaze to the table.

She wasn't a fan of jazz music. Normally, she could just ignore it, but in that moment, with the heavy pause between the two of them, the sound of the saxophone grated against her nerves.

"I tried to resist the call. She drove me mad *for days*. Vivienne didn't understand the suffering. I could only fight my dragon so much. Eventually, he won and answered. Aimee is my true mate. I am powerless against fate. We all are. We must do as fate commands."

As heartbreaking as it was to hear the pleading in his tone, Alisa understood what he meant, having experienced the torment that was heat. Males must go through something similar. While logical, the story still bothered her.

She'd known others who'd been fathered by unmated pairs. They spent time with their kin and co-parented. There was a sense of family. Only, he had turned his back on his child.

"What could my mother have done to warrant you abandoning your egg?" Furthermore, what had made her grandmother blame him for her mother's death at the hand of the witches? There had to be a missing piece, and he could tell her.

Again, he winced.

"You knew I hatched," Alisa reiterated.

He nodded, and a spark of anger lit in her chest. A faint stream of smoke came from her nose.

"You were aware I existed?"

Again, he nodded. The flame of annoyance grew inside her.

"So what happened?" His lack of detail aggravated her. She needed answers. Why couldn't he just be forthcoming?

Offering her a tight-lipped frown, he sat back. "This isn't a first-time meeting conversation."

"*Excuse me*?" He just told her how her mother had tried to trap him into a chosen mating with an egg. Now he thought he could back off. What the hell went on between them?

"I wanted to establish..." he paused, as though trying to find the right word. "If you'd allow it, I'd love to get to know you too, but this isn't the time or the place to discuss—"

"Well, I need to know your side of the story. All I've been told is that you left and witches murdered my mom because of you. What happened?"

Motioning for her to lower her voice, he glanced around, clearly nervous about the proximity of human ears overhearing their conversation.

Leaning over the table, he spoke in a hushed tone. "Your mother had years to explain it to you. She didn't die when you were a baby."

His words fed the inferno of rage inside her. "And you had three decades to show up in my life."

"If you knew—"

"Tell me!"

He shifted in his seat, and his gaze darted around again.

If people stared, she didn't care. She'd never been this close to having the answers to her past before. She wasn't about to let a few humans interfere.

"It's not something to explore out in public like this." He gestured around them.

"Oh, please. You've mentioned plenty that shouldn't be discussed in mixed company." She folded her arms over her chest. The deep, dark secret should be out in the open. It'd been hidden long enough.

He wouldn't make eye contact with her. Instead, he let out a heavy sigh and clenched his jaw.

"I suffer every day because of what you did to my mother. The Ember Witches have shunned me. I don't have the elixirs."

"But you have the tattoo?" he asked in a desperate tone.

She narrowed her eyes at him. "Of course I do," she growled. "I got that as a baby. Before her *death*."

She hoped her words would hit home with him. As far as she knew, Duncan Hayes caused her mother's demise. He should feel her pain.

Instead, he nodded, seeming relieved.

What the actual fuck?

"But nothing else. They want no part of me. What did my mother do? It had to be something awful."

"It wasn't one thing."

"At least tell me what made you walk away and never look back."

The muscles on either side of his jaw twitched as he tightened it. He balled his hand into a fist on the table. "You aren't ready."

"Don't tell me what I'm *ready* for. You don't know me. Remember?"

"Fine." His eyes widened with frustration, and smoke billowed from his nose. "She murdered our egg—me and my mate's. She couldn't handle what fate decided and thought destroying our hatchling would bring me back to her."

All the oxygen in the room vanished, snuffing her angry flames. Her dragon bellowed in her mind. That couldn't be right. Her mother wasn't—only pure evil would do such a thing.

"Then, when that didn't work, she demanded the witches undo my mating. When they refused because they don't have that sort of power over fate, she decimated them too. Vivienne was absolutely insane. If it wasn't for the child witch, who knows how far she would have gone. You happy now?"

"No." Alisa's voice was small. It almost sounded like it came from someone else.

There was no way her mother would do that. In the nine years Alisa had with her, she'd been nothing but loving and doting. She'd never hurt a baby, let alone an egg.

"I'm sorry," he whispered. "I shouldn't have just blurted it out like that. I should have—"

"You're lying."

His shoulders slumped as though the realization of what he laid on her bore down on him. "I wish I was."

He had to be.

"It's not true!" Alisa shouted this time. That wasn't the kind of dragon her mother was. He was covering his own ass by making her mother look evil.

"Alisa," he hissed, glancing around.

"Ma'am?" A concerned barista approached cautiously, flicking his gaze between the two of them.

"I'm fine." Alisa snorted and waved him off.

Rising to her feet, tears in her eyes, she had enough. She couldn't sit there and listen to this stranger soil her mother's name anymore.

"I told you that you weren't ready."

She shook her head, her vision blurring as she cried. "You're a liar."

It was all she could think to say.

"Please, sit down." He stood as well. "We can work through the past. You aren't Vivienne."

She'd had enough. Never in a million years had she imagined this to be what her father would say to her during their first conversation.

Either way, it didn't matter. He told her his version of the story and he chose to lie. She never had to see him again. Rolling her shoulders back, she lifted her chin, summoning all the dignity she could. "Goodbye, Mr. Hayes. Thank you for your time."

She couldn't keep the venom out of her voice. He was a stranger to her. She should've never looked for him. It was better to wonder what had happened than to have his lies.

With her head high and pain in her heart, Alisa stormed out of the bougie coffee shop. She had gotten what she came for—shitty answers from a horrific father. She shouldn't have expected anything less.

43

9

DECLAN

*G*olden scales, like nothing Declan had ever seen. Beautiful magnificence lay beneath him.

Squeezing his eyes shut, he slammed his fists into the heavy bag.

Bam. Bam. Bam.

Beads of sweat poured down from his brow as his heart raced.

Her plush, supple body writhed when he buried himself deep inside her tightness. She was a golden goddess.

Growling, he opened his eyes and resumed hammering the bag. It'd been hours since he'd left the mating grounds. Why was she still on his mind? He gave none of the females he'd rutted a second thought. This one, though, she wouldn't evaporate from his brain.

"You bit a female dragon at the mating grounds?" Gideon's incredulous words resounded in his mind an hour after his friend left the gym.

The bite didn't matter. She didn't return it. Declan wasn't marked. He'd know if he had been. Gideon was the idiot who'd mated with someone accidentally. Declan had more control over himself and his dragon than that. Besides, Declan had learned from his friend's mistake.

The image of her shuddering around his cock burned into his brain. With her riding him reverse cowgirl, he didn't get the opportunity to see her face. Next time.

No.

It wouldn't happen again. That wasn't how any of this worked.

His dragon had been restless since they'd left. The beast practically paced inside his mind, grumbling. Something was off. He just couldn't put his finger on what.

Maybe his beast was upset the sow had spoiled his good time with the lionesses?

He had no choice. She wouldn't shut up. The dragon within him had some nerve being agitated about any of it. It'd been his godsdamned idea. Declan would've been just fine with the two felines.

The beast inside him groaned. He could feel the animal rolling his eyes.

Fine. That wasn't it. But the night hadn't exactly gone well.

He and his dragon had pissed the golden dragon off so badly she stomped away. The deed was done. They'd rutted. There was nothing left to do. The sow stopped calling. What the hell did his dragon want to stick around for? To cuddle?

Declan snorted so hard it was practically a laugh at his own thought. Dragons didn't do that shit. They fucked and got the hell out of there. He had no idea why his beast was suddenly sentimental.

After he dropped his sore fists, his shoulders slumped, and he hung his head. Letting out a heavy breath, he gave up. There'd be no amount of exercise that would distract him. He'd have to endure flashbacks of the previous evening for a while, he supposed. Maybe he just needed a shower and a good night's sleep or something to get her out of his head and her scent off his skin.

Stepping away from the boxing equipment, Declan uncoiled the tape from his wrists. He dropped his weary body onto a bench and deposited the wraps into the trash before he reached for his bottle of water.

She was golden. They were the rarest of all dragons. Of course, she lived rent free in his mind. It wasn't about the bite and everything to do with her coloring. His beast liked shiny objects, and there was nothing shinier than golden dragon scales.

He wished he'd snagged some as a memento before he left the mating grounds. No one would believe he'd rutted a golden dragon. Then again, he wouldn't go around bragging about it.

Dumping the rest of the water on the back of his neck, he hoped it would wash away the heat she'd left in her wake. He couldn't be sure, but something inside him said he'd rutted a fire dragon.

He never wondered what kind of dragons they were before. Fire, ice, water, wind, what did it matter? They were the same—sows desperate to sate their heat. None had been golden before, and none of them had burned into his memory.

She was different.

His dragon huffed as though agreeing with the thought.

She was his.

She wasn't either of those things.

Okay, maybe the first. She battled harder than the rest. For half a second, he really thought she'd get the better of him. Not that it'd ever happened before or that he'd have allowed it. He would've fought to his death rather than suffer the loss of honor of a female denying him the right to rut her.

Fine! They agreed on one subject. She was different—golden and tough. He needed a good night out on the prowl to rid her from his thoughts. After he finished work, he'd hit the bars. Once his beast got a taste of some felines, he'd forget about the dragon that glittered.

The animal inside him snorted.

He would. It's the way it always had been before. Why would this be any different?

Alisa

Steam rose from the tub as Alisa eased her body into it. She'd healed enough to fly back home, but the soreness in her shoulders clung to her. Not to mention, the bite mark he'd left ached.

Stupid asshole.

She hoped her lavender bath oils and the fizzing bomb she'd dropped into the water would help soothe her.

Lying back, she folded a thick washcloth before she covered her eyes with it. She needed to wash away the previous evening and the disappointing conversation with her father. How dare he lie about her mother.

There was no doubt her mom had done something egregious. Alisa understood that. The Ember Witches wouldn't extend a shunning to kin if it wasn't something horrendous, but what Duncan Hayes had claimed was too far. There was no way the woman who'd loved her so deeply could be capable of such things.

She'd spent nine years with her mother. Alisa had a good sense of her character. Nothing was violent about her. She never so much as raised her hand to Alisa. Her mom would never have smashed an egg. It wasn't possible.

But why would Duncan lie?

She'd thought meeting her dad would answer all her questions. She'd finally know the truth. Unfortunately, he'd just given her more quandaries. She was no better off after meeting him than she was before.

VRRRR. VRRRR. VRRRR.

Groaning, she let the washcloth fall from her face and into the fragrant bathwater.

VRRRR. VRRRR. VRRRR.

The only people who had her number in the city were her co-workers and her boss. She'd gotten a job bartending at a shifter-owned bar pretty quickly after she'd arrived. That was one positive about the shifter community, as much as they bickered among themselves, they always took care of one another.

VRRRR. VRRRR. VRRRR.

But it was barely noon. There was no way anyone she worked with would look to contact her.

VRRRR. VRRRR. VRRRR.

That meant only one person would call her.

Letting out a heavy sigh, Alisa leaned over the edge of her claw-foot tub and tapped her phone. "Hi, Grandma."

"Lee Lee." Her grandmother sang her nickname. "So good to hear your voice."

Alisa rolled her eyes at the faux concern in her grandmother's tone. "It's barely been a week."

"I know, but you're so far away. Manhattan is riddled with humans, and I watch the news. Anything could happen."

She couldn't help but snicker. "I'm fine."

"You don't sound fine."

"I'm in the bath." Alisa sat up a bit more and pulled her knees to her chest. "So, you're on speakerphone."

Her grandmother clucked her tongue on the other end of the line. "What's the matter?"

"Nothing."

"Don't lie to me. You only take baths when something is bothering you."

"It's nothing."

"Leeeee." Her grandmother drew out her name.

Grumbling to herself, Alisa shook her head. She might as well tell her. Her grandmother would be relentless if she didn't. "I found him."

"Who?"

Alisa rolled her eyes. Her grandma knew damn well who. "My father." She humored the woman.

"Ohhhh."

"It didn't go well."

"I told you it wouldn't. He's a horrible man."

With her shoulders slumped, Alisa couldn't help but nod. "I just never expected him to be a liar."

"He left your mother for someone else. Of course he is," her grandmother snapped.

Ever since Alisa had left the café, she'd replayed his words in her mind. His explanation of what went on didn't sit right, yet he'd sounded so sincere. She didn't want to believe him, but as of now, he'd been the only one to offer her any details.

"He said some things," she started. "I just, they make little sense to me."

"I'm sure. He likes the sound of his own voice."

"They never mated," Alisa stated.

"They were chosen mates," her grandmother affirmed. "They never got around to a ceremony or anything, but I saw their markings. He selected your mother, and she accepted him. That is the best dragons can ask for these days."

So, they *had* bitten each other. One thing confirmed. "How long does it take to officially become a chosen mate?"

Her grandmother sighed. "I don't know. Each couple is different. For some, it's months, like your grandfather and me, but others, well, it can be a rougher road. Some couples are just more compatible than others. We are at the whim of the fates. Your mother and that snake in the grass were together for so many years. They were most certainly official. Did he say they weren't?" she asked but didn't pause long enough to get an answer. "Of course he did. Any justification to up and leave his egg and his mate."

"Kind of. He said they tried to be chosen mates," Alisa offered, feeling suddenly defensive of her only living parent. "But it didn't take. He said he found his destined partner."

"Impossible," her grandmother refuted. "He was already mated. There was no way he would have heard the call. Besides, it's impossible for dragons. Destiny has abandoned us. The odds he met his true mate are so slim they aren't even worth considering."

Alisa furrowed her brows. "So, there's no way their chosen mating could have not, I don't know, not solidified?"

"You don't understand. *Years.* They were together for *years.*"

"I thought bonded males couldn't rut other females. Like their stuff doesn't work."

Alisa struggled with this detail. As far as she understood dragon mating and rutting, once bound, male dragons couldn't rise to the occasion with any female other than his mate. As such, *if* her father and mother were bonded, and it was solid, he wouldn't have been able to create another egg with a different female. His parts just wouldn't have worked.

Her grandmother sighed. "What did he tell you?"

"Was there another egg?" Alisa pressed.

Nothing.

The silence had Alisa's mind race. For six weeks, Duncan hung around with her mother—even though he wasn't ready to have an egg. He witnessed Alisa being lain, but then he ran off with another female? A male who sticks out a laying wouldn't just book it. He couldn't if he were truly mated.

"Grandma. Tell me the truth."

Silence. Instead of words, she heard huffing on the other end of the line.

Why wouldn't she answer? "If there was another egg, you and I both know they weren't mates, chosen or otherwise."

"They were mates," her grandmother insisted.

Not that she wanted to defend Duncan—especially after what he'd said her mother had done—but facts couldn't be denied. A mated male dragon could not create eggs with more than one female—only the one he'd bonded with could inspire him. Unmated males could, in theory, father plenty before settling down.

"No, they weren't," Alisa whispered as the full impact of her own words slammed into her chest. They weren't bound to one another, which meant there could have been another egg. That meant that Duncan might have spoken the truth.

"What did my mom do?"

10

DECLAN

With Gideon almost always with Ella, Declan was left with a friendship vacancy. Thankfully, the night his friend met his mate, said mate had a wingwoman. Felicity, the cute witch-in-training, stepped up to fill Declan's companionship void. Perfect timing. Stuff like this gave him faith the fates knew what they were doing.

All hail fate.

Humming to himself, with a bounce in his step, he carried a sack filled with guacamole, chips, tacos, and rice with beans. The other bag had a handle of tequila, limes, and margarita mix. It may have been Wednesday night, but that didn't mean he couldn't celebrate Felicity's birthday.

Birthdays were Declan's favorite occasions of the year. There was nothing better than barhopping with his friends and getting free drinks. He swore that birthday alcohol never gave a hangover. As a shifter, with advanced healing, hangovers weren't usually a concern, but he stuck with his theory anyway.

Tonight, they'd enjoy tacos before heading out to meet up with Ella and Gideon. Everyone would drink themselves into a stupor to celebrate their friend.

Once he reached the apartment, he lifted his fist to give the door a good knock. His humming progressed to mumbling the wrong words to a song. He wasn't even sure if he sang one or a mash-up of a few. It didn't matter. He was pumped.

"Coming!" he heard from the other side of the door and sniggered at the sexual innuendo.

While he waited, he did a little shimmy shake of a dance. It would be fun. It'd been a while since all four of them got together. Plus, he needed something to get the golden dragon off his mind. It'd been a godsdamn week. Something had to give. A night out drinking with his friends and possibly hooking up with some felines ought to do the trick nicely.

The door opened, and Declan jumped, startled at the sight. "What the hell?"

She'd wrapped a towel around her head, covering her long black hair as though she'd just gotten out of the shower. It looked like moist paper was stuck to her face, but it had eye holes and a cutout for her mouth. She wore a tank top and brightly colored fleece pajama pants with fluffy slippers. This was *not* the outfit of a woman ready to hit the town and celebrate her birthday.

"Are those tacos?" she asked, reaching for them.

"Why aren't you dressed?" he asked, allowing her to take the sack of food as she stepped aside to let him in.

Following him into her apartment, she dug through the bag. "Why would I be?"

"We're hitting the town for your birthday, remember?" He went to the kitchen and set to unpacking the drink supplies. "I figured we could pregame a little before we went out."

"Oh shit," she said, rounding the counter. "It *is* my birthday, isn't it?"

She sat on a stool and unpacked the containers.

"How do you forget your own birthday?" He placed his palms on the countertop and leaned forward a bit.

She lifted a shoulder and opened the guacamole, then the bag of fresh-made chips. A grin lit up her face when she inhaled the scent of the food.

"I don't know. I'm adopted and sort of stopped caring about it when I was in high school. Thinking about how the people responsible for my existence were dead made it seem wrong to celebrate my life."

"That's heavy."

"Hmm." She popped a guacamole-covered chip into her mouth. "It is what it is."

Frowning, he considered their agenda for the evening. "So, you *don't* want to go out tonight?"

Canceling plans would suck. Sure, he could party and snag a hookup on his own. It might even be easier, but he looked forward to having the group together again.

But the night wasn't about him. He did his best to quell his disappointment while waiting for her answer.

Leaning over the counter while crunching, she studied the bottle of tequila. "On a Wednesday?"

"It's the best day for festivities." He turned to look through her cabinets for a shaker. "Fever is closed to humans," he said of the nightclub that was owned and operated by shifters. "So, we get the place to ourselves. Every week, Jason gives drink specials to different species."

Once he found it, he spun and faced her with the metal drink mixer raised in victory.

"And I may or may not have convinced him today should be witch's day." He winked.

"Huh." She sat back in her seat. "I never knew that."

"Why would you?" he asked as he twisted the top off. "You pal around with humans. It's not like they're invited."

"Wait! Can Ella get in?" Felicity frowned. "Never mind. She's probably working any-way." Never had disappointment been so palpable than in that moment.

Good thing he could save the day.

He chuckled and reached for the tequila. "Of course. She mated Gideon. The com-munity is well aware. They'll make an exception, and I already got her to agree to come."

Hopefully that would convince Felicity.

As he poured the ingredients into the shaker for a strong margarita, she glanced down at her attire. "I suppose I can pull myself together."

"We don't have to *really* celebrate. I was just using your birthday as an excuse to round everyone up," he offered as he retreated to the freezer for ice.

"No, it's fine," she said on a sigh. "My twenty-first was the last time I really got into my birthday, I think. And that was only because Ella made me. So yeah. Let's party."

"Whoa now," he mused as he filled the shaker with ice. "I didn't get you a gift or anything. So, I'm not sure how much of a party this is really going to be."

Finally, she laughed. "You brought tacos and margaritas. Those are presents."

"Fair point," he agreed, opening the final cabinet to retrieve glasses. "Then we will consider it a proper birthday gathering. Do you have one of those cardboard pointy hats?"

She tapped her finger on her paper-covered chin. "No, but I think I have a tiara somewhere."

"Why do you have a tiara?" With the margarita glasses found, he pulled the cap from the shaker and filled them.

"Every woman does." She grinned and took the first glass. "Let me wash my face. I don't want to get this mask in the tacos."

He swore he heard a little squeal come from her as she scooted off the stool and headed toward her bedroom. She may have forgotten their plans, but at least she seemed excited now.

With a margarita in one hand and a chip in the other, he resumed his humming from earlier. Munching away, he enjoyed the deliciousness gracing his tongue. It wasn't the same place they'd gotten tacos on the night they met, but it would do. This guacamole was better.

As he took a sip of the drink, he danced a little, and something occurred to him. Pausing his movements, he cocked his head to the side. When she left the room, he hadn't taken the opportunity to ogle her caboose.

Not in a creepy way. He just did it when women walked away from him—he checked out their backsides. There was no staring or drooling. It was a mere glance of appreciation.

Either way, he hadn't done it.

Swirling the bright-green drink, he pondered his lack of booty watching. Had she crossed the threshold from potential bedmate to true friend? They'd hooked up a little the night they met. It was nothing serious, just kissing and heavy petting. Tacos had distracted them.

Chuckling, he flipped open the container of fish tacos. Apparently, tacos were their thing. Until that moment, Declan had always considered Felicity a potential hookup. If the two of them were in the mood and available, he'd just assumed they'd get down.

But something changed. Somehow, somewhere along the line, their relationship became more than a mere sexual attraction.

"Cool." He nodded to himself as he scooped the guacamole on a chip. "I'm maturing."

It felt like the dragon within him rolled his eyes. What was his problem?

11

ALISA

Existential crisis aside, bills still needed to be paid. Grappling with the atrocities Alisa's mother *might* have committed would have to wait until after she finished her shift at Fever. She'd only just started working at the shifter-owned nightclub two weeks ago.

Alisa had been a bartender for nearly a decade. She'd worked for all kinds of owners—humans, witches, vampires, etc. However, when she was employed by a shifter, things seemed to go smoother. The pay was the same, the tasks were identical, but the vibe was better.

When she learned about Fever, she knew that'd be where she'd apply for a job while she stayed in Manhattan. However long that would be. With her month-to-month sublet apartment, she could take off whenever she had to. There was something freeing about knowing nothing tethered her to this city.

Trotting down the stairs of her building wearing comfortable sneakers, black leggings, and an off-the-shoulder T-shirt with a backpack slung over her shoulder, she wondered if her time in the area had already ended. She had gotten what she came for. She had met her father. Yet something still felt unfinished.

An image of the teal dragon flashed through her mind.

Nope. Not that. She quickly shut down that line of thinking.

It probably had to do with how she left things with Duncan. She came to get to know him. That wasn't what happened. So, of course, everything was up in the air.

Would she ever be able to fix that?

Shaking off her thoughts, she headed over to the mailboxes. That was a question for another time. Especially considering he'd dropped the most unbelievable bombs on her.

Refocusing on the tiny doors, she took a deep breath. Not that she expected any letters or anything, but she hated when it got loaded with junk mail. That was her pet peeve—seeing a mailbox stuffed with useless garbage. What a waste of paper.

Pausing, she stared at her box. Stuck in the door's seam hung a red envelope. An air of foreboding wafted toward her. An eerie sensation crawled up her spine. Swallowing the irrational feelings, she cautiously stepped toward it.

This wasn't how the mail person delivered letters. She'd emptied the box the other day. There was no way it was full already. So, whoever left this envelope hadn't done it through the postal service. Wasn't that illegal?

She eased it out of its crevice and flipped it to see if it had been addressed. Maybe it wasn't meant for her. It could be for the person whose name was actually on the lease. That had happened before.

Alisa Roberts was written in a fancy calligraphy. What in the name of the gods was this about?

Slipping her finger under the flap, she tore open the envelope. Inside, she found an invitation and a business card.

This was over the top.

Skimming the invitation, a knot formed in her gut. When did he do this? Wait. Had he left this before?

Turning, she peered over her shoulder—half expecting to see a Land Rover at the curb. Guess not.

Blowing out a breath, she returned her focus to the card. Her father had formally invited her to a family dinner at his place. He enclosed his business card, with a number handwritten on it, in case she wanted to call him.

Tapping the letter to her chin, she considered it. If he delivered it before their coffee, the invitation might no longer be valid. She hadn't exactly walked out on their little meetup on good terms. Then again, he may have put it in her mailbox while she was in the bath. But why? She'd stormed out of the coffee shop. It would take some serious balls to leave an invitation after their encounter.

They'd literally just met. Who printed single invitations like this anyway? So unnecessarily formal. Rich people, apparently.

Closing her eyes, she dropped her hands to her sides. This was drama she didn't need. Then again, logically, by opening the can of worms that was meeting her father, she'd be foolish to expect there wouldn't be stress. She'd done it to herself.

Tucking the invitation and business card into her backpack alongside her change of clothes, she decided it was something she could worry about later. Or another day. The dinner wasn't that evening. It was at the end of the month. Really, she had time to decide.

For now, she needed to focus on getting to work.

Declan

Three margaritas barely touched Declan. Felicity, on the other hand, was practically human. Witches were the closest species of supernatural beings to humans. They didn't have enhanced senses. No inhuman strength. No enhanced speed. No quick healing abilities. The magic which flowed through them was far more focused. Shifters, vampires, and the like possessed more global magic in the form of abilities. Witches got spells.

He supposed it was a fair exchange.

Her giggling and stumbling meant he made a strong margarita. Perhaps too potent for the little witch. He needed to remember that next time he mixed a drink for her.

"Happy birthday to me," she slurred with her arm looped around his. "I live in a zoo."

He chuckled as she leaned into him. "That's not how that goes. It doesn't even rhyme."

"It's my birthday. I'll sing it how I want," she snapped playfully.

Declan patted her head. "Okay, princess."

"That's right," she said as she reached for her tiara. It had been straight, but after she messed with it, not so much.

Snickering, he rolled his eyes. "When did you become such a lightweight?"

"Intermittent fasting." She groaned.

"Why?" He wrinkled his nose. Felicity had a lean frame with small breasts and a perky ass. She didn't need to drop any weight. Hell, he wasn't sure where she thought she had it to even lose.

As he considered her body type, he couldn't help but compare hers to the golden goddess. The female dragon was probably the same height but had much more meat on her bones. She had thick thighs and supple hips. The memory of his fingers pressing into them and pulling her down onto him made his cock twitch and his dragon swoon.

Nope.

He couldn't think about that right now. He had to focus on the birthday girl and the night ahead of them. Especially since Felicity seemed to lean into him to keep herself from falling over.

"I'm writing an article." She broke into his thoughts. That was right. She was a journalist, after all.

"About how stupid intermittent fasting is?" he suggested.

She snickered. "Pretty much."

"I guess all those tacos didn't help your research," he mused.

She rested her forehead on his arm and laughed.

As they approached the line to get into Fever, Declan's pocket vibrated. With one arm supporting his friend, he used the other hand to retrieve his phone. After a swipe and a few taps of his screen, he unlocked it and read the message.

Shaking his head, he rolled his eyes. "They're running behind," he informed Felicity as he tucked the phone back in his pocket.

She blew out a breath. "Of course they are. Ella gets nowhere on time."

"She works too hard," he said as they headed straight to the front of the line.

Everyone waiting was human. They wouldn't get in. Jason probably should put something out about the club being closed for a private party to avoid all the humans.

"Mike!" Felicity squealed as she released Declan and took off toward the Kodiak bear bouncer.

Arching a brow, he watched her fling herself at the other male. He hadn't been aware she knew him that well.

"It's my birthday!" she announced once the bear caught her.

For someone who didn't celebrate her birthday often, Felicity sure seemed into it, in the moment.

"Again?" The bouncer sounded amused. "Happy birthday."

Declan shook his head and smiled. She should be this happy on her birthday. A blip of pride budded in his chest as he considered himself responsible for her mirth. Sure, it was margarita induced, but at least it got her in a quality mindset. He'd take what he could get.

"Will you be in the VIP section later?" she asked as she ran her fingers through the security guard's thick beard.

Ahh. That made sense. Declan hadn't considered reserving a table. He hadn't thought they'd stay too late. It was the middle of the week, but a place to set up shop away from the crowd was a good idea.

Hindsight was twenty-twenty and all that. Oh, well. They'd still have a good time.

The bear shifter chuckled as he carefully placed her back on the ground. "Nah. The door. Then the floor a bit."

She offered him a pout. "Okay." She turned to Declan. "Come on, let's go find a table."

Dipping his chin, he offered a polite greeting to the bear shifter as he followed Felicity. The security guard's eyes turned dark and narrowed slightly as Declan passed. Oh, the shifter had a thing for the witch. How adorable.

Little did the bouncer know, but he had nothing to fear in Declan. He and Felicity were just friends. Unfortunately, there was no hand gesture or signal he could offer to let him in on the situation.

Though, with her hand wrapped around Declan's, there was definitely a different message being sent to the bear as she tugged Declan through the door.

Once inside, thundering bass and flashing lights swallowed them. House music muffled the conversations happening around them, and bubbles danced in the air. Bodies writhed on the dance floor as servers carried trays of beverages.

This was the perfect environment to celebrate someone's birth. The positive energy radiated through the room and vibrated through his chest. He loved this scene.

What was that? His dragon perked. Who caught his attention? He prayed the two lionesses from the other evening wouldn't show up. That would be a whole new level of awkward he didn't need to deal with. He doubted they'd give him a second chance.

Did his dragon just snicker at him? What an asshole.

Felicity continued to drag him through the crowd to find a table. All the while, something tugged at his senses. The overwhelming aromas of shifters of all varieties, vampires, fae, and witches combined. That wasn't it. It was more distinct—more familiar.

He knew that scent but couldn't place it.

Ocean spray. Amid the myriad of fragrances, the saltiness of the sea tugged at his dragon. Who was it?

12

ALISA

Wednesdays were insane. Alisa had seen nothing like it before. Jason, the owner of Fever and her boss, opened the nightclub to just supernatural beings. It felt like every nonhuman creature in the tristate area had shown up. *On a Wednesday*, no less. It had to be the best marketing gimmick she'd ever seen, and it was all word of mouth. Jason hadn't spent a damn penny, yet the place was jam-packed with humans waiting outside.

She probably should be thankful. Being that busy kept her thoughts from meandering to her father.

And the teal dragon. The feel of his hands on her hips—the way he made her shudder. Don't go there.

Stop. Her mind and her beast needed to behave.

She shouldn't think about him. They did what they instinctually had to do. She took her measures to prevent the consequences of such things. She needed to shove him out of her brain and get on with her life. If he hadn't been such a violent dickweed, she probably would have forgotten about him already.

Her attention should be on her night and finishing this cosmopolitan.

The bar was packed. The dance floor was wall-to-wall writhing bodies. A plethora of scents mingled in the air. Fae, witches, vampires, and shifters of every variety were about. It made for a delightful bevy of smells swirling around her. Though most prominent was almond.

Odd. She hadn't smelled this potent of almond since the mating grounds.

The teal dragon.

Stop it, she internally warned herself and her dragon.

She shook her head again. All roads needed to stop leading her mind to the teal dragon. She needed to focus on the present.

Wait. How much vodka... dammit. She dumped the drink and started over, quickly making the cosmopolitan before taking another order from the faes in front of her.

The VIP section was jammed with vampires and fae—they were the snootiest of the nonhumans. They clung to a monarchy type system. So, everything with them was about status and station. Vampires rarely ordered anything, but the fae always asked for the most random and exotic drinks.

On a night like this, she was accustomed to well drinks, beers, and the occasional martini. Unfortunately, these Manhattan supernaturals were above the common order.

They wanted mojitos and pisco sours. What in the name of the gods was a pisco sour? She had to ask Rick, the closest of the three other tenders at the bar. It had egg whites in it. Ugh. The last thing she needed to deal with were eggs.

"Hey," Hailey, one of the coyote shifter women serving, called. "I need three mojitos, two Jack and Cokes, a whiskey sour, and a Corona."

"Got it," Alisa called as she shook the ice-filled shaker a second time. "I'll finish these and get yours going."

"You remember how I told you sometimes we get dragons here," Hailey said as she ducked under the service bar.

Grinning, Alisa rolled her eyes in amusement.

Everyone working at Fever had been excited when Alisa arrived. Some of her co-workers actually thought her kind was extinct or mythical. Hailey, on the other hand, knew of other dragons and begged to introduce Alisa to them.

Dragons preferred wide-open areas. In their beast form, they were massive. Not only tall but wide. They had tremendous wingspans. So they needed space. Cities, like Manhattan, were far too cramped for shifting. It definitely posed challenges. So it made sense to Alisa that her own kind were scarce in the area.

"Well, one of them is here." Hailey shimmied her shoulders as she took it upon herself to muddle the mint leaves for the mojito while Alisa finished the order.

Alisa cracked the shaker and poured the pisco sour she just made between three glasses. "Oh, cool."

She hadn't been interested when Hailey had brought it up and was less so now. She'd come to Manhattan to find one dragon in particular, and she'd accomplished that. Meeting any others would be a waste of time. She had enough on her plate. With her luck, the one shifter Hailey craved to present to Alisa was her own brother.

If she wanted that, she'd just go to that fancy family dinner Duncan had invited her to. There wasn't a chance in hell Hailey had known her father well enough to introduce him to Alisa.

He didn't seem like the type to go club hopping. With a mate at his side, a true mate nonetheless, he had no reason to socialize. They weren't social creatures.

Alisa offered the drinks to the women waiting for her and collected the credit card for payment. She trotted over to the register to open the tab.

"He's over there," Hailey said, tapping Alisa's arm.

"In a minute," Alisa said as she worked with the touchscreen.

Once she got the card open, she placed it in a glass. The first copy of the receipt printed, and she scribbled a brief description of its owner on it before stuffing it beside the card. The other receipt came, and she offered it to the woman with a smile.

Done with that, she took a deep breath and started on the next order. "Jack and Coke," she repeated as she grabbed glasses and filled them with ice.

"Look," Hailey insisted.

Groaning, Alisa glanced in the direction where the server pointed, and her inner beast perked.

With her hand resting on the bottle of whiskey, Alisa's heart stopped. Her dragon did flips in her mind. It was all she could do not to let her jaw drop.

The teal dragon.

There he was in his human form, standing at a table a mere fifteen feet from her. No wonder she couldn't get the scent of almond out of her nose. The bastard who bit her was right there!

"He's kind of..." Hailey bumped her shoulder.

Snatching the whiskey from the speed rail, Alisa glared in his direction. "I don't think so."

"What?" Hailey balked. "Are you sure you're looking at the right guy? The one in the blue button-down. He's with the drunk witch in the tiara."

"Yeah, I see him," Alisa grumbled, unable to tear her eyes off him. Her inner beast thrashed her tail at the mention of the woman beside him. They both noticed.

Who was that? A witch? He had the audacity to be with a witch? The dragon inside her snapped her jaws. Alisa snorted and grabbed the soda gun to fill the glasses with cola. She needed to stifle that blossoming jealousy real quick. There was no time for that.

"I bet you he'd abandon her for his own kind. Coyotes can't resist each other." Hailey reached into the cooler and pulled out the Corona.

Alisa scooted around her and placed the drinks on Hailey's waiting tray. Gritting her teeth, she couldn't take her attention off the woman beside the teal dragon. It was enough to turn her dragon green.

This was ridiculous. She had no reason to feel like that. "I really couldn't care less. I'm not looking."

She took the pre-muddled mint and began making the three mojitos. Her dragon flipped her tail while Alisa glared at the woman laughing with *her* male from the mating grounds.

The beast inside her needed to calm down. It wasn't that serious.

"Well, you don't have to be in the market. Sometimes, the market is into you."

Alisa scoffed at the server's unrestrained optimism. "Not everyone is looking for a mate."

"It's our biology. Until we have one, we're always on the hunt."

"Maybe with coyotes, but not dragons," Alisa lied through her teeth.

"I dunno," Rick chimed in as he rocked his shaker back and forth. "It's definitely the case with panthers. It's like an itch we can't quite scratch until we do."

Alisa's beast shrieked inside her mind as the witch beside the teal dragon rested her hand on his arm. Alisa's grip on the bottle tightened. The witch threw her head back and laughed. The sound carried over the crowd, and it felt like nails on a chalkboard. Alisa slammed the simple syrup down.

"Oh my gods," she huffed. "Just because he is a dragon and I am a dragon doesn't mean we're mates."

Neither did the fact that he bit her—the fucking asshole. Because he couldn't restrain himself, he'd driven her dragon insane. Jealousy burned in her chest. Her beast continued to thrash about and all Alisa could do was wince while she made cocktails.

"There are other dragons." Her words were meant not only for the shifters beside her but for her inner beast as well. Hopefully, someone would be convinced.

Hailey and Rick exchanged glances with tight lips.

What did they know? They weren't dragons. Dragons were different.

She moved the three mojitos to the tray before starting on the whiskey sour. "I get dragons are a novelty here, but really, it's not something either of you need to worry about."

Rick's eyes widened, and he turned to exit the conversation.

"I wish you would consider talking to him," Hailey mumbled as she ducked back under the service bar.

"I'm a little busy here."

Everything she had to say to the teal dragon had already been said. That dickwad tore into her shoulders, which were still sore as hell, and he'd *bitten* her. There was nothing left to discuss. If anything, she needed to stay away from him before her dragon got any ideas.

The beast was already doing cartwheels in her mind because of his proximity. She had a crush on him. Which, Alisa could guess, was fair. Teal was their favorite color. His scales had been quite beautiful. She should have saved some. If she wasn't so pissed, she might have.

Wait.

Did she just consider collecting pieces of him? What the hell was that about? No one kept another dragon's scales. That was just weird. Gods, meeting her father had really set her out of sorts.

13

DECLAN

"**D**o you think they'll make it?" Felicity asked, out of breath.

Ella and Gideon had said they were on their way over an hour ago. He'd done his best to help celebrate her birthday by dancing with her and buying their drinks since they'd arrived, but it was clear she really wanted to spend time with her best friend, Ella. He probably should be insulted, but he understood.

"Yeah. I do." He shrugged and reached for his beer.

Felicity wanted her lady friend. If nothing else, his sisters had taught him the importance of females having female friends. Some things he'd never be able to relate to as a male buddy. It wasn't like he could go with her to the bathroom.

Considering Gideon had been scarce, Declan would bet Ella wasn't around as much for Felicity either. While she had stepped up to fill Declan's void, he hadn't exactly been able to do the same. He enjoyed his space, and Ella technically lived with Felicity, but he'd doubted she slept there much. He wasn't about to move in with the woman to replace Ella.

Unfortunately, it was the nature of mating. Once it happened, the couple became consumed with each other. They lost track of social commitments. Declan witnessed it firsthand when his half sister, Scarlett, mated with a bear.

Actually, when was the last time he'd seen her?

He should really call and check in. She might have a kid on the way or something. How would that even work? Would she have an egg or a bear cub? He'd heard it could go either way. Mixing species like that caused all kinds of chaos.

After he took the last sip of his warm beer, he inhaled deeply. That salty sea air scent nagged at him. It had his inner dragon pacing. Glancing around, he tried to sort out what was around him. It was like the nightclub was saturated with the scent. While Manhattan was an island, it never smelled this much like the ocean inside the nightclub before.

"Are there any seagull shifters here?" he asked.

"What?" Felicity slammed the empty bottle of water she'd finished. She'd switched to water pretty quickly after they'd arrived.

Three margaritas and two mojitos had her on the verge of sloppy. No one wanted a sloppy drunk on a night out—birthday girl or not. Thankfully, she agreed to the switch and had actually gotten better with the water and the dancing.

"Seagull shifters. Have you noticed any?" he repeated.

"How would I know?"

"I thought witches could sense that kind of stuff. Obviously, you can't smell them, but magic. I thought you'd just *know*."

She peered at him with an arched brow. "Better witches than me can. I'm seriously barely an apprentice. Like I can tell shifters are around, but I don't have a clue what kind."

He frowned. This was why he needed Gideon around. It'd be a tremendous help if someone else could sniff things out.

"And I'm not even sure I'm that much of an apprentice anymore. Ever since the complete debacle at the Mountain Gala, Auntie Josephine has been scarce."

Declan snorted. "She threw Gideon's mate off a cliff. It's not something a shifter can forgive easily. And even if the human part of him did, the dragon definitely won't."

Felicity blew out a breath. "I was pissed too, but Ember Witches have a responsibility none of us can ever comprehend."

"Yeah, our animal half doesn't understand nuance like that." Declan picked up his empty bottle. "You ready for another drink yet?"

Felicity's shoulders slumped as she leaned over the table. "What time is it?"

"It's birthday time!" Ella shouted as she approached. "I've got shots!"

Felicity's eyes brightened as she straightened. The smile spread across her face as she bounced up and down. "You made it!"

Ella deposited four small glasses filled with clear liquid on the table. "I wouldn't miss the rare opportunity where you agreed to celebrate your birthday!"

The human female absolutely reeked of fresh sex. Declan shook his head. Of course, rutting delayed their arrival. "Where's Gideon?"

Holding up one shot, Ella nodded to Felicity. "At the bar," she said, thumbing behind her with her free hand. "He's getting you two whiskeys or something. So, I have these for us. Happy birthday, Felicity!"

As the two women clinked glasses and threw their heads back to take their shots, Declan shifted his focus to the bar area.

At first, the sea of supernatural beings blocked his view of the bar. Wednesdays were the most popular night to go to Fever. It was the only nightclub in the area that catered to nonhumans. It may happen one night a week, but for those few precious hours they got to truly be themselves and not have to worry about humans were priceless. The stress of masking evaporated among proper company.

Ella was a different story. She didn't count. The entire supernatural community of Manhattan knew about the human who mated to the dragon. She got a pass.

As though to prove their comfort with her presence, there was a faerie on the dance floor, letting it all hang out—blue skin, pointy ears, wings, and everything.

Dragons couldn't do anything like that. There simply wasn't enough room. They had to stick to the sanctity of the mountains.

Someone stepped aside, and he got a view of Gideon's back and someone else. While his friend chatted with Rick, the panther shifter bartender, a female hustled beside him. The silver shaker shook above her head while she leaned down to hear an order. Declan couldn't make out her face, but the view he had made his beast flail about in his mind.

Was she a lynx or something? He definitely preferred felines. Who was it?

When Gideon stepped aside to head toward the table, Declan got a good look at her. A chill rippled through his body as his scales threatened to erupt. His dragon roared and drowned out the techno-house music. Salty sea air slapped him in the face.

She flicked her dark-brown hair, and his gaze darted immediately to her shoulder. The shirt she wore had a wide neckline and it revealed where he'd bitten. The dragon stomped his feet and thrashed his tail in dissatisfaction.

Damn. She was just as beautiful as a human in the glow of the blinking lights from the dance floor as she had been at the mating grounds.

"The golden goddess," he murmured.

"What?" the two women closest to him asked in unison.

Blinking, he shook his head, trying to tear his attention away from her. He'd almost done it until she shifted her gaze, and their eyes clashed. His chest fluttered, and his cock stiffened to full attention, nubs and all.

Godsdammit.

"I've seen that look before," Gideon said as he stepped right into Declan's line of sight.

A growl rose in his chest. The dragon didn't care they were best friends. He'd just blocked his view of the golden dragon. Declan clenched his jaw and did his best to rein in his beast. The animal within him didn't have control—the human half did. The beast needed to calm the fuck down.

"There are lionesses around, aren't there?" his best friend mused.

"Ohhh." Ella chuckled.

Declan forced a smile as his friends joked at his expense. Again, he reached for his beer, forgetting it was empty.

Gideon winked and offered him a half-filled glass of brown liquid. "Dalmore."

"Thanks," Declan said, accepting his favorite scotch whiskey.

"He said something about gold," Felicity offered. "Are lionesses normally blondes?"

Gideon furrowed his brows. "No. Not really. Lions, like their full-on cat counterparts, are originally from Africa and India, so..."

"Oh." Felicity dipped her chin.

"They have a lot more melanin." Gideon swirled his glass.

"But." Ella peered between the two men. "Aren't dragons Irish?"

After exchanging a glance, the two men chuckled. Gideon was the definition of Caucasian and quite Irish. Declan, less so despite his Gaelic name.

"Dragons are everywhere. So, we come in many colors." Declan took a sip of his scotch, savoring the flavor rolling over his tongue.

The beast inside him wailed. He needed to get it together.

After swallowing, his eyes found their way to the bar again. Scanning back and forth, he frowned. One. Two. Three.

Usually, four tenders worked during Wednesday nights.

Where had *she* gone?

14

ALISA

Alisa's heart raced. Her body burned. The dragon screeched in her mind, making concentration impossible. Not only had she just served two of the most expensive whiskeys in the bar to what had to be her half brother—he was the spitting image of Duncan, only younger—but to make matters worse, she'd just established eye contact with the teal dragon.

Godsdammit.

She couldn't breathe.

Space.

She was about to hyperventilate. There wasn't enough room for that. Behind the bar was far too cramped.

"I need fifteen," she called over her shoulder as she jetted toward the service bar to get out of there.

"Now?" Rick balked.

She didn't respond. Instead, she ducked under the counter and headed for the door.

Fresh air had to help.

At least, she intended to get to the door. Her dragon fought with everything she had against her mental walls. Somehow, the beast had gained control of their legs. They headed straight for the middle of the crowd.

The human half of Alisa couldn't stop it.

Gritting her teeth and tightening every muscle, she battled. She had to cool down. Getting closer to the teal dragon would only do the opposite. Her skin tingled. It felt like flames danced beneath the surface. Scales threatened to burn through.

"I only brought up gold because the dragon I encountered at the mating grounds last night was golden." His voice was clear as a bell over the blended conversations of the bar. "I'd seen nothing so magnificent, and I suspect she's here."

Her heart fluttered, and her beast practically did backflips in her mind. He considered her to be magnificent. What a word to use. No one had ever said anything like that about her before.

Stop it!

She couldn't fall for silly bullshit like that. It was the same jerk who bit her without permission. He tore into her shoulders. He was an asshat, not sweet.

Rein it in.

Alisa couldn't see him through the two vampires dancing in front of her, but she could hear the lust in his words, and it sent a shiver through her. The memory of their coupling at the mating grounds flashed in her mind.

She had to stop moving. Getting closer would only make things worse. Actually, she should turn the fuck around.

"Where?" the teal dragon's friend asked.

Wait.

No way. For fuck's sake.

"The mating grounds," the teal dragon admitted.

She groaned to herself.

Of course, the guy beside the dragon who made her weak in the knees had to be Alisa's half brother. Why wouldn't they know each other? This was her own personal hell, after all. Manhattan was most definitely Alisa's personal underworld at this point.

Unable to peel her gaze off the male from the mating grounds, her dragon swooned and slapped her tail left and right. The animal within Alisa didn't give a shit about her kin being near.

Alisa had to get the hell out of there. She couldn't stay so close to him. Her dragon was infatuated. She couldn't be trusted.

That stupid bite, half-mating bond, was far too potent for her liking.

"Dragons come in gold?" asked a human, who, based on her scent, was most definitely mated to Alisa's half brother. She stank of him.

Move feet.

Alisa couldn't get her legs to work. Her dragon was desperate to go to him. Her human wanted to run out of here. So, with the two entities inside her battling for dominance, she stood frozen with her hand on a table filled with empty drink glasses for support.

"Yeah." The teal dragon nodded. His gaze was fixated past his friends and toward the bar area.

Her heart lodged in her throat at the realization that he was looking for her.

"She was spectacular."

Another compliment had her dragon spinning circles in her mind.

Her beast slammed her body against the mental barriers. Alisa physically stumbled and bumped into someone.

"Sorry," she mumbled, collecting herself.

"Gold dragons are the rarest of our kind," Alisa's half brother chimed in. "I thought they were gone, honestly."

Almost but not quite.

He would know. Alisa snorted to herself. Because of her father, they'd only become that much rarer. Rage flared in her chest and tangled with the dragon's angst. Her blood boiled as she narrowed her eyes. The table shook in her hands as she squeezed it, fighting the beast from continuing toward the male from the mating grounds.

This wasn't the time. And it most certainly wasn't the place.

"Oh my god!" the witch in the tiara exclaimed. "This is my favorite song."

Alisa had paid little attention to what the DJ had played before, but she tuned in at that moment. "Tricky" by Crazy Frog. The magic bearer couldn't be serious. This tune was awful.

The magic bearer snatched the human's hand and squealed while bouncing up and down. "Come on!" She waved at the surrounding men.

Alisa's eyes widened when the teal dragon tore his gaze away from the bar to laugh and go along with the one in the tiara.

How dare he!

He just stopped looking for her. She was right in front of his face, and he ignored her.

She could almost forgive her half brother for not noticing his kin near, but the dragon who had bitten her? No. He should have found her. Jealousy surged through her, and her dragon screeched bloody murder in her mind.

Unable to control herself, Alisa let out a low roar of her own. Several of the surrounding shifters glared as she curled her fists. Her scales slid against one another beneath her burning skin. She didn't have much time.

Her dragon wouldn't stay inside much longer. The beast raged and flung her full mental weight against the barriers keeping her imprisoned in the human consciousness. She had to let the animal out. Bumping up against the point of no return, Alisa turned and fled the bar.

Open space. She had to find somewhere she could shift safely.

Her transformation came on fast. An agitated dragon would do that. Alisa barely got to the top of the nightclub before her dragon erupted from her body. She didn't even want to think about what would happen if she got caught in the street.

Taxicabs, people walking by the scaffolding, all of it would have been crushed because her beast was an impatient little wench. Sometimes, being a massive dual-being was more of a pain in the ass than it was worth.

Especially when her dragon forced the transition so quickly only to perch herself on the roof and shout her head off. This wasn't the mating grounds. Why the hell was she screeching like that? If she wanted to call a male, then she should fly to Ireland. Why had she sat her fat ass down right there and hollered?

She better not attempt to summon the teal dragon. Alisa never went back for seconds—not even in dragon form. One and done. He had his chance.

The witch's scent would be all over him since the magic bearer was all grabby and touchy-feely. Drunk little bitch. The last thing Alisa wanted was to smell another female during a rut. It was the ultimate slap in the face.

At least if they were at the mating grounds, if a male had been with another female, the flight there would blow the stench off. But hanging out mere feet from where the teal dragon was, no doubt, grinding up on the stupid witch wearing the tiara—ugh. He'd definitely still reek of her.

Hidden in the recesses of her beast's mind, she did her best to attack the mental barriers holding her in. She had no desire to see that asshole again. Her shoulder still fucking hurt anyway. And he had his chance. She didn't care if he was the last unmated male dragon on the planet. She'd rather be single for the rest of her life than to rut him again.

Alisa kicked and screamed inside her mind.

Move. Just fly somewhere else.

If her beast insisted on doing this mating call thing again, then she could at least give another dude a chance. Don't half-ass it. Go where the mating stuff was supposed to happen. Don't hang out in the city.

She wanted nothing to do with the friggin' teal dragon.

After one last bellow, her beast spread her wings and bent her legs. Finally. She shoved off and took flight.

However, instead of heading northeast, toward Malin Head, her dragon headed south. What the hell? Where in the name of the gods was she going now?

And she really needed to shut the fuck up. Alisa felt a migraine coming on.

15

DECLAN

That sound. The feral deep rumble ricocheted through Declan's body. He'd heard it before at the mating grounds. His dragon turned within his mind, and his human head followed the direction. She growled just as she had at Malin Head.

The golden dragon had her back to him and seemed to shove those around her out of the way.

He'd know her anywhere, from any angle. "I'll be right back," he said to his friends, unsure if they even heard him.

Felicity had Ella. She didn't need him anymore. This was more important.

Hold up.

He stopped in his tracks, having only barely stepped away.

She *rejected* him. She left *him* at the mating grounds. He hadn't gone after her then. Why the hell would he chase her now?

Glancing over his shoulders, he watched as Felicity and Ella raised their arms and whooped. Gideon bopped behind his mate, sipping at his whiskey. He wasn't dancing with them so much as he monitored his woman, as any decent mated male would.

Pinching the bridge of his nose, squeezing his eyes shut, Declan was tempted to release his own roar. The dragon within his mind thrashed around, desperate to follow the female from the mating grounds—the golden goddess. But why?

Alright, he could admit he might have half mated her, but she hadn't returned the sentiment. By that logic, he shouldn't chase after her. No matter how much his beast demanded it. She'd vetoed the idea. No bite from her meant no sealed mating bond.

Just half a one that would fizzle out in time.

If he let it.

However, when he tried to return to his friends, his legs wouldn't move. The animal in his mind huffed before barreling into his defenses. His skin cooled, and ice chilled his blood, threatening to make his scales erupt.

The dragon half of him wasn't playing.

He longed to go after the sow from the mating grounds.

Too bad she didn't want—

Eeeeee. He stiffened as the sound ripped through his skull.

No way.

Eeeeee. His breath caught in his throat.

Glancing around, Declan sought anyone else responding to the sound. Would Gideon sense it now that he was mated?

No.

Declan knew that already. He'd gone deaf when he mated with Ella. There had to be another dragon. Anyone would do. The hollering was so loud. Surely, someone else would answer it.

Eeeeee. He flinched.

He knew better. No other dragons lived in Manhattan. That call was intentional. It was for him and him alone.

The desperation in the cry throttled through him, and his legs moved toward the door. His dragon seized control somehow.

What in the ever-loving fuck was going on?

Eeeeee.

"I'm coming," he growled as he stormed out of Fever.

Holding his head, Declan emerged from the club and stumbled slightly. Out of the side of his eye, he caught the confused expressions of the human patrons, hoping for admission. The bear bouncer beside him raised an eyebrow but otherwise paid him no mind.

The shrieking of the female dragon's mating call tore through his skull. It was so loud his ears rang. As the chill rippled through his body, his scales pressed against his skin. His dragon needed to calm the fuck down and wait for him to find a suitable space for the shift.

Eeeeee. Declan reeled as she cried out to him once more.

What was this sow's problem?

Seriously. She'd just been in the same building as him—mere feet away. If she wanted him, she should've walked up to him. He'd have had no problem talking to her. She didn't have to pull this shit and turn tail to run, only to scream for him. It made no fucking sense. Not to mention, she had the worst timing ever.

First, she ruined his night with the lionesses. Now, she interrupted his friend's birthday celebration. There were better ways to see him again. All she had to do was ask. This stupid mating call bullshit needed to stop.

Eeeeee. His dragon thrashed and whipped his tail against Declan's mental barriers, causing him to trip. He curled his fingers around the scaffolding pole to prevent a fall. Pain rocketed through his arm as the first cracks of his limb realigning for his transformation began.

Godsdammit.

This wasn't the place. He needed space, and Central Park was too far away. Scanning the streets, desperate, he spotted a parking garage.

That would have to do.

Using his preternatural speed, he bolted for the rooftop level. It wasn't ideal. There might be humans around up there, but he didn't have a choice. His dragon had surpassed impatient.

Taking steps two and three at a clip, Declan ascended to the highest level. Panting wildly with his heart threatening to burst through his chest, he fell back against the door to the rooftop. Curling his talon tipped fingers into a fist, he let out a loud roar in time with the shrieking bitch's call.

It didn't matter how quick he went from human to dragon, the transition was agony. Every muscle tore. All of his bones broke. Ice covered his body before the dragon burst through his human form. Shards of frozen water pelted the sedans and SUVs around him.

The massive animal snapped his head to the left and spread his wings. The tip of his limbs scraped along a minivan beside him and made the alarm screech into the night.

Perfect. If Declan didn't get a headache from the horny sow yelling for him, he sure as shit would have one from his clumsy oaf of a dragon.

16

ALISA

In all of Alisa's grown-ass adult years, suffering through her heat, summoning males to sate her, never had her dragon flown to anywhere else but Malin Head—the mating grounds. What the hell was her beast doing?

There was also something different about her cries. Alisa couldn't put her finger on exactly what about it had altered. Maybe the pitch? The tone? It wasn't like she bellowed words. It was a roar-like sound that came from deep within the beast.

This time, it sounded strange.

Everything about this call was odd.

It had to do with the teal dragon. She knew it in her bones. Her shoulders burned from the wound he'd inflicted upon her—at least that was what she told herself. She refused to believe it had to do with his bite.

As he said, she hadn't returned it. Therefore, it meant nothing.

Which was a lie.

She didn't want to think about half mating and what that would mean. Right now, she needed her dragon to shut the fuck up before he actually showed up stinking like the witch.

Ugh. The idea made her blood boil, and her beast snapped her jaws in similar irritation.

Internally, her human half hissed at her dragon half. Externally, her beast plopped her fat ass on a mostly bare, undecorated rooftop. The smell of tar and bird shit filled her nostrils.

A makeshift, dilapidated pigeon coop stood off in the far-left corner. Beside it was a lone summer lounge chair, bleached from the years of sun exposure. The fabric of the cushion was torn in several places with the stuffing exposed.

She knew this place.

Glancing around, Alisa attempted to gain her bearings. This wasn't just a random building. This was the roof of her own apartment.

The fuck?

As the beast let out another shrill cry, the human half sat back in her mind, befuddled. The rickety shack filled with pigeons squawked as feathers flew. The shrieking had to have stunned them. Why would her dragon call the teal dragon there?

She leaned forward slightly, considering the possibilities. Would the roof be able to support the weight of *two* dragons? One had to push the limits of the infrastructure. What would *two* do?

Oh shit.

This was about to get superbad.

As though to punctuate that point, the distinct swishing of dragon wings flapping caught her attention over the settling cooing birds locked in their pen. Her beast turned toward the sound.

She screeched again. This time, he returned her call.

A loud boom roared from the teal dragon as he approached. Humans might believe it a clap of thunder, but not a single storm cloud floated in the sky. Again, feathers flew from the startled pigeons. The feral rumble from the male pummeled her body, causing her to quiver in anticipation.

Instincts kicked in.

Godsdamn heat.

Her scales burned as fire flared in her core. The mere sight of the teal dragon made her own beast swoon and the bite he'd left behind on her shoulder burn in the most exquisite way. Magma flowed through her veins as arousal blossomed.

Her cycle would be the death of her.

The closer he got, the higher her internal temperature became. Were she a thermometer, the mercury would have exploded through the top when he hovered near the edge of the building.

With his talon-tipped feet grazing the ledge, his dragon cocked his head to the side as though studying her. Alisa's beast, on all fours, swayed her hips back and forth to tempt him with a dance.

What the hell?

Never in her life had her dragon done a *dance* for a male. Typically, she screamed for one. When he showed up, they fought a bit. If he conquered her, he won the right to rut her.

But not tonight. Far too many oddities had presented themselves. Something had changed. Alisa clung to her denial and refused to acknowledge the obvious, which itched at her brain.

By swishing her tail, seduction radiated off her in waves. Her beast would entice this male one way or another. Whether Alisa, her human half, agreed with it or not. It didn't help that the dragon's need for him pulsed through her veins and crept into Alisa's human half's judgment.

Would one more romp be such a bad thing?

Yes.

Yes. It absolutely would be a horrendous idea.

Just as the teal dragon's claws dragged along the ledge, he came forward. The familiar cracking and popping of bones and joints realigning sounded through the night. His beautiful scales *tinked* as they dropped to the ground. Alisa fought the urge to scurry over and collect them.

He didn't flinch.

He didn't cringe.

His intense, lust-filled stare held her in place, making her core quake, betraying her human side. There'd be no resisting.

As his maw shrank, his gaze held hers. His toned human form took shape from beneath the dragon. Gone was the hardened armor of his dragon. Smooth human skin covered rippled abs and his toned chest. His Adonis belt, the deep V below his belly button, drew her eye.

Alisa's mouth watered at the sight of his thick, nubbed dragon erection protruding from his pelvis. A pearled bead oozed from the tip, flaunting his arousal for her.

She couldn't help it when her tongue slid along her lower lip.

Her need reached a new peak, and she mentally fanned herself. Both she and her dragon gulped at the sight.

He was absolutely stunning in the moon's light. Any female worth her salt could agree to his splendor in both forms. Why did he have to be such an arrogant prick?

"The full moon makes your scales glow."

Well, shit.

The appreciation in his voice stroked her ego and her growing desire for him.

He stepped toward her and into the beam of light from the motion-censored lamp above the door to the roof of the apartment building.

Her pussy pulsed. A flush blossomed in her chest and burst up onto her dragon cheeks. She doubted it was visible, but the inferno blazed throughout her body and her human consciousness. There was too much beauty in that dragon shifter male.

A deep shadow settled in the depths of his brown eyes. When his pupils enlarged to hockey pucks, his entire expression turned from appreciative to sinister ferocity. His fingers wrapped around the shaft of his thick dragon dick.

"I can smell your arousal. You're about to learn what that does to me."

Her breath hitched, and her heart skipped a beat. Her sex blazed greedily for him. The whimper that escaped her lips had nothing to do with the pain rocketing through her. Broken bones and torn ligaments weren't the cause of her moaning.

It was the want in his eyes, the yearning in his tone—it exacerbated her own excitement. Decadent hedonism fogged her brain through her shift.

Rutting the teal dragon male became her sole purpose.

17

DECLAN

The golden dragon's erotic scent saturated the air. It dominated every one of Declan's senses. He'd been pissed when he left the nightclub, but the anger evaporated with each inhale and spawned into a greedy desire for her. Nothing would stop him, or his beast, from filling her with his dragon cock.

As her glittering scales melted from her shrinking form, he pumped his hand over the buds of his beastly dick. Squeezing his fingers over the tip, he used his own pre-cum to slicken his thickening erection.

Never in his life had he grown so hard or his balls been so heavy. But the sight of her supple bare skin drove his dragon mad. His mouth watered at the idea of tasting her. Tight nipples accentuated her full breasts. They were more than his hands could handle, but he was determined to manage. The flare of her hips begged him to grab them so he could pull her against his body. His chest rumbled at the sight of the thick black lines of the dragon head tattoo decorating her plush abdomen. A grin spread as he ran his tongue along his lower lip while he drank in the length of her perfect legs.

She was magnificent. No other words could describe this sow—his female.

Glancing around, he sought somewhere clean to lay her down. They stood on the tar-covered roof of an apartment building. Pigeons cooed inside a shack to his left.

Ahh!

There was something he could use.

The lounge had a metal frame, which meant it would hold up against the pounding he was about to dish out. The shabby cushion, though torn in a few places, looked like it would offer some reprieve during their intense rutting.

"There." He pointed to the lounge chair with one hand and stroked himself slowly with the other.

Internally, his dragon snapped his jaws, desperate to take hold of the golden female before him.

Momentarily, she shifted her gaze away toward the outdoor seat. When it returned to him, her dark eyes blazed with a hedonistic need matching his own. Her body flushed, and a fresh wave of arousal filled his nostrils. She tested his restraint.

"Now," he growled.

She shivered.

"You summoned me here," he reminded. "To rut."

A moan slipped past her lips, but she didn't move.

Releasing his cock, he stalked toward her. In five long strides, he closed the gap between them. At six foot eight, he towered over her barely five-foot-ten frame. So, he had to crouch slightly to meet her. With his face mere inches from hers, he inhaled her salty, fresh ocean scent. Lifting his hand, he curled his fingers beneath her chin and guided her to meet his gaze again.

"Declan," he whispered.

Confusion decorated her perfect features.

"My name. So you can scream it."

A snicker of challenge escaped her, and he lost it.

Both of his hands found her full hips. Digging his fingers into her soft flesh, he reveled in the gasp that escaped from her. Her eyes widened but smoldered. She wasn't objecting—merely surprised.

Careful but still forceful, he tossed her to the cushioned lounger.

Before she could collect herself, he dove between her legs and wrenched her thick thighs apart. "I've wanted to taste you since the mating grounds."

Dipping his head down, he didn't wait for her to protest. The scent of her potent permission drove his inner dragon mad, and his cock strained painfully for her. After one deep inhale of her musk, he spread her lower lips with his fingers and flicked his tongue against her soft wetness.

Her hips bucked, and she lifted her ass up, offering her dripping pussy for him to feast upon. Declan swirled his tongue. He explored her intimate folds before dipping into her well of heat. Her flavor burst on his tongue, and his balls tightened.

When her legs tensed and her groaning elevated to cries, he dipped two fingers deep inside her pussy and pulled his mouth away. Grazing her thighs with his teeth, his dragon pushed him to bite.

Not yet.

"Say it," Declan urged as he curled his fingers upward, searching for her G-spot.

"What?" she panted as her body quaked.

"Say it. Or I *will* stop."

Whining, she flailed, slapping her hands on the ratty cushion.

He slowly withdrew his fingers while using his thumb to circle her sensitive, engorged bud. Biting his lower lip, he fought the urge to tease it with his tongue. Grazing it with his digit would have to do.

"Please!" she begged desperately through gritted teeth.

"You know what I want," he taunted, circling her clit ever so slowly.

Her body rippled, and he reached down to stroke himself again. His dragon roared in his mind. He wanted to take the sow. The beast within him didn't need to play any more games. Her taste lingered on his tongue, but the animal inside him craved all of her. Not just a sample.

"Please," she repeated, her desperation intensifying.

"Say it," he commanded as he applied pressure to her nub.

Her back arched, and she fisted the cushion. "Declan!"

That was all he needed. "Good girl."

With lightning speed, he lifted himself. Positioning the head of his dragon cock against her opening, he didn't hesitate before he plunged himself deep inside her.

A delightful heat encircled him. Her walls clamped down on him like a vise, squeezing his dick to the point of pain. Declan saw stars. Without thought, he gave in to his beast and pummeled her pussy—thrust after thrust he drove himself inside the golden dragon as she screamed his name over and over. Each time amped him up further.

She shook violently beneath him, pushing him closer to insanity.

Her hands found the globes of his ass, and she dug her fingers in as though urging him to go on. Hissing, he tucked his head into the crook of her neck. Her skin scorched his lips. He couldn't get enough. She was the most addictive creature he'd ever encountered.

Claim her, his dragon demanded.

Opening his mouth, baring his teeth, he then sank them into her shoulder, biting her again, in the same spot he had at the mating grounds. Blood graced his tongue just as his orgasm exploded from him.

Declan didn't stop or slow down. His hips rolled, and he continued to piston in and out of her tight sex. They were a perfect fit.

Lapping at her fresh wound, his dragon reveled in the flavor of her blood.

Panting, he turned and pressed his lips to her ear.

"Do it," he whispered.

There was no fighting it. He'd seen what a catastrophe denying a mate could be. That wasn't his fate. If his dragon wanted her, he'd do it. He'd give in. This was his sow.

"Do it." Declan tilted his head and offered his neck to her. "Or I'll stop."

Slowing his pace, he dragged his still erect cock out of her. Teasing her opening, he circled his hips, leaving just the head inside her.

"Do it, and I'll make you come." Leaning on one elbow, he reached between their sweaty bodies and sought her clit. He found her swollen bud and traced it with his index finger.

Twitching beneath him, she moaned deeply. "Please," she whimpered.

"Do it."

When he pinched her clit between two fingers, he slammed his dick in as deep as he could. She jolted under him, and her open mouth found his shoulder.

Pain seared through his body, and his balls vibrated. Again, he withdrew and hammered deep into her over and over.

She bit down harder, and he left his body.

Her thighs tightened, holding him deep inside her. Her pussy walls squeezed his cock before rippling around him. Declan's head spun, and his body trembled as he emptied every bit of dragon seed inside her.

The most intense orgasm of his life barreled through him. He was on a different plane of existence, soaring to heights he never knew existed.

Just as he approached the moon, he collapsed over her and returned to this world.

The golden goddess's head fell back, and reality crashed into him while the two of them panted to catch their breath.

They'd just officially mated with each other.

18

ALISA

Usually, Alisa got quite warm when she slept. It was a natural consequence of being a fire dragon. It only became a problem in the summer or when the air conditioner broke. Waking up in a puddle of her own sweat was never a good time.

That night, her rest had been the most comfortable of her entire life. She hadn't gotten too hot. It was like she slumbered beside a block of ice. She'd never been more content and could've slept for ages like that.

Then someone cleared his throat.

Fluttering her eyes open, Alisa squinted into the rising sun. There was a heavy arm over her and a leg curled up over her hip.

Who had the audacity to ruin her slumber?

Shaking her head and using her hand to block the sun, she peered up at the person who had woken her.

"Oh shit," she muttered.

Reality slapped her right in the face.

The man who tended to the pigeons in the coop beside them—yes, them, which was another problem—stood before her with his arms crossed over his chest.

They were bare-assed as the day they were hatched. While totally normal in the shifter community, they were in mixed company. The pigeon keeper was human. He definitely wasn't accustomed to two people naked on his lounger.

Two.

Gods. They hadn't merely rutted, they'd *slept* together. She'd never shared a bed—or a lounger, for that matter—with a male. And the bite. What had she been thinking? Her world tilted on its axis.

She'd returned his marking.

One problem at a time.

Deal with the human first, then sort out what the hell the two of them had done the previous night.

"You don't have to stare," the teal dragon, Declan apparently, said as he cupped her breast, covering them from the view of the pigeon keeper.

"I have to feed my birds," the man replied incredulously.

"Then do it. We aren't in your way," Declan hissed.

"I'm sorry," Alisa chimed in. She didn't want to move and reveal herself fully to him. It would only make matters worse. "We hadn't intended to—"

"Bah." The pigeon keeper waved his hand, dismissing her words. Shaking his head in derision, he shuffled past them toward the shed of birds cooing eagerly for their seed.

Covering her face, Alisa let out a heavy breath. What had she done? How was she supposed to handle this? How could she manage *this* with a human within earshot?

"You smell divine in the morning," Declan whispered into her neck as he nuzzled against the bite he'd left—the brand, the mating mark.

They'd mated.

Her heart picked up pace.

"Could you not," she huffed.

Gone was the asshole from the mating grounds. The insensitivity he displayed there was replaced with compliments and tenderness. Alisa didn't have time for that nonsense.

He squeezed her tighter. "Not enjoy my mate? That seems counterproductive."

He came right out and said it. It didn't matter that she hadn't been entirely on board or that they were strangers to one another. Okay, knowing one another wasn't a requirement for mating, but either way, she wasn't ready for this.

"Where is your self-respect?" barked the pigeon keeper as he exited the coop. "Can't you at least wait until I'm gone to canoodle?"

"If you don't like it, don't look," Declan chirped back on a chuckle as he softly kissed the mating mark on her neck. "Eyes on your own paper, old man."

Alisa reached over her shoulder as best she could and shoved his head away. "Stop."

Still holding her but loosening his grip, Declan recoiled slightly and peered at her with confusion decorating his beautiful features.

In the morning light, she had a better view of him. Full lips, high cheekbones, and deep, dark-brown eyes. He was beautiful.

Stop it.

She couldn't notice things like that. It didn't matter that he was attractive.

"What's wrong?" he asked.

The door to the apartment building slammed shut. The pigeon keeper had finally given them privacy.

"*Get off. Get off.*" Alisa shoved Declan's arm and leg away from her. Scrambling to her feet, she allowed the anger to heat her blood.

He peered up at her, blinking several times and wearing an innocent expression.

If she wasn't so pissed, she would admit he looked adorable. Shaking her head, she planted her hands on her hips. "What the hell did you do?"

"Me?" He placed a hand on his chest as he sat up. His semi-erect human dick dangled between his spread thighs.

"Yes!" She ripped her gaze away and stared into his eyes, trying to maintain her ire.

Her dragon, on the other hand, had other ideas. She wanted to fixate on his manhood, recalling the orgasms he'd bestowed upon her with it.

"You took advantage of me."

His brows rose. "*Excuse me?*" He stood his full height, almost a foot taller than her.

Damn, he was glorious.

No. She couldn't think such things. Pressing her thighs together, she did her best to ignore her boiling core. "I'm in heat. My dragon and I cannot be trusted with decisions in that state! You bit me and made me bite you back! You forced this mating."

"Are you new?" he asked in utter exasperation. "Forced? Took advantage?" he repeated, shaking his head. "The purpose of your heat, the mating call, all of this"—he gestured in a circle—"is to find your mate! And that's me! What did you expect me to do?"

"Show restraint."

"You expected a dragon to hold back when fate brought him his mate?"

"I had some."

"Not last night, you didn't."

"*You made me!*"

He threw his hands in the air, laughed, and turned away from her. "You have got to be kidding me." He inhaled deeply before whipping around and facing her again. "Listen, I never expected to mate to a dragon, either. I honestly thought I'd be the dragon head of a lion pride or something, but this is what fate gave us. We can't reject that."

"*I'm in heat*!" she repeated. What didn't he understand about this? "You can't deny a dragon in her heat an orgasm and expect her to make rational decisions—especially big ones like mating!"

"News flash." He closed in on her.

Her breath caught in her throat when he paused inches from her and jammed his finger in her face. This shouldn't turn on her. She should rage. Maybe bite that digit. No. That would definitely lead them down the wrong road. Anger. Fury. She had to hold on to that. If she didn't want to end up like her mother, she needed to cling to the anger and push him away. Her stupid dragon shouldn't be fawning over him right now. *They were mad at him.*

"When you're in this"—his fingertips skimmed up her sides—"state, *I* can't control *my* dragon either. He does what he desires."

Quivering, Alisa held her breath. Son of a bitch. He wasn't playing fair. Her stomach fluttered, and her pussy slickened.

"We are dual beings. Our beastly halves, our dragons, are driven by their instincts—our instincts." He dipped his head so his lips grazed her ear as he spoke. "We cannot fight what destiny has gifted us. We are mated."

Her nipples were painfully tight. The humidity between her thighs was ridiculous. He exploited her vulnerability. Instincts and fate be damned.

"I can smell your agreement." His lust-filled words licked her core.

With her inner dragon practically rolling over in submission to him, Alisa scurried away. She couldn't handle this. She didn't need this.

"Where are you going?" he demanded.

Without a word, she twisted the knob and pulled the door to her apartment building open. If she stayed there another second, she'd allow him to bend her over once more. The thought made her knees buckle.

She squeezed her eyes shut. This wasn't the appropriate time. She wasn't ready for this.

They'd bite each other again. Their bond would be that much stronger. She couldn't have that right now. She couldn't deal with him. Fleeing, she used her preternatural speed to descend the stairs to her apartment.

Thankfully, he didn't follow her. She couldn't trust herself, or her now-whining drag-on, around him much longer. What had she done?

19

DECLAN

With his mouth agape, Declan stood alone on the roof of an apartment building, bare-ass naked in the morning sun. She couldn't be serious. Twice in two days, she fled.

What the actual fuck?

Yeah, he wasn't exactly thrilled about the idea of fate denying him his fantasy of a threesome with two feline shifters, but it was what it was. Having a dragon mate was the dream. Hell, every dragon he knew thought it was impossible to find exactly what destiny had given them.

If *he* could accept that, then what the hell was *her* problem?

Obviously, she'd been looking for a mate. She took the stupid releaser and went into heat. He forgave her before because he assumed her to be new to the entire process, but seriously, he could only excuse so much.

She bit him back. They were mated. Only death could separate them now. It wasn't complicated. Every shifter on the planet was familiar with this. How could she deny any of it?

He'd be damned if he'd live a life of misery because his mate rejected him without a good explanation. He wasn't sure what that could be. The idea of her with another male sent ice shards through his veins. *They were mates.* Another man couldn't have her. She was made for him. Destiny decreed it.

Gritting his teeth and curling his fingers into fists, he glared at the door.

Maybe he *should* go after her. He let her flee before. That'd been an obvious mistake. Maybe it was time to stand and show her what having a mate meant. His eye twitched when his inner beast thrashed his tail against his barriers.

His dragon wanted to chase their mate.

Declan took a deep breath.

No. He needed to give her space. If she took the releaser recently and this was her first experience with seriously seeking a mate, he shouldn't push her. It was one thing to fantasize about the idea of a mate, but the reality could be hard to process.

Besides, it wasn't like she would bed another male. Mates didn't work like that. Once the bond formed, they wouldn't be able to achieve satisfaction with anyone else.

Then again, that hadn't stopped Gideon from trying. Stupid asshole. With the way the golden dragon behaved, she might be as dumb about the facts of mating. He and his beast growled, infuriated at the foolish idea she'd attempt to rut another male because of her own denial. That couldn't happen. He'd rip the male to shreds.

Shaking his head, Declan rubbed his temple. What the hell was he supposed to do?

He needed time to consider their mating. It wasn't just happening to her. His life had changed as well. Running his hand along the back of his head, he smirked at himself. He'd never hear another mating call. Random females wouldn't interrupt him anymore.

That'd be nice.

Nodding to himself, he let out a heavy sigh. It was like a weight had lifted off his shoulders.

Hold up.

If he was officially mated, that meant he got his ice. Excitement ran through his veins, and his dragon did a flip inside his mental confines. As his destined other half, she should have gifted him ice when she bit him.

Glancing around, he considered how he could test it. Well, first things first, he couldn't do anything in human form with ice. He'd have to shift. Mentally, he poked at the beast inside him. When the creature snapped back at the prodding, he chuckled to himself. He was definitely ready to spread his wings and try this out.

But he couldn't do it there—not in the city anyway. He needed to go somewhere with space. Giddy with excitement, he strolled toward the ledge. While his mate grappled with the idea of being his, he would flex his wings and play with ice. Worse stuff existed in the world.

Yes, he knew from when Gideon and Ella mated that rejection could be painful, but he could endure that. If his best friend could muddle through it, Declan could do the same. And maybe it would put the nonsense in perspective for the golden goddess. A little pain hurt no shifter for too long. It was a small price to pay for what fate had planned for them.

Patience. Good things came to those who waited.

He could give her a few days to sort her shit out. It wasn't like their dragons would keep them apart for too long. The next time he saw her, and there would be one, he'd make sure they discussed everything. He'd lay it all out on the table, and she'd have to explain to him any hesitation she had.

They'd work through it. Considering they were fated mates, they had no other option.

As he looked out over the city during the bustling morning hours, optimism bloomed in his chest. He had a mate—a dragon mate. He was living the dream. The only hiccup being her acceptance of it. That should be easy enough to figure out, but for now, what he wanted was to breathe ice.

Closing his eyes, he summoned his dragon. Considering he was naked as the day he was hatched, and he couldn't just walk around the city in that state, the only choice he had was to shift and fly to the mountains. He left clothes at his parents' house for just this occasion.

When a mating call was particularly desperate, he could shred through his clothes during a shift. So, he needed a backup plan. With acres of property in the mountains of Colorado, dragons were guaranteed not only space but privacy while in their beastly forms. He was due for a visit with his family anyway. Might as well kill two birds with one stone.

He couldn't wait to announce that he'd mated a dragon. Maybe his family could help him brainstorm how to convince his sow it was a good thing. They might even have ideas as to her hesitance. Either way, he was about to have an excellent visit with his family.

20

ALISA

ot that locking the door would do anything, but Alisa did it anyway. If Declan, the teal dragon, wanted to, he'd get in. A mere apartment door wouldn't prevent it. Covering her face, she fell back against the wall.

What had she done?

She lacked control of her body. The beast inside her did it. But that didn't matter. It was done. She'd mated him.

A mate.

A fated mate.

A dragon fated mate.

Shouldn't she be excited about finding her destined other half? She had what so many like her desperately desired, but she wasn't in a state to accept this. Why did it overwhelm her? She hadn't gone to Manhattan to find a male. Well, not in that sense. Yes, she went there seeking her father—who was, in fact, a dragon male—but she hadn't gone there for a mate.

Sliding down, she landed on her ass and pulled her knees up to her chest. Resting her forehead on them, she wrapped her arms around her shins.

This wasn't the right time.

As though to mock her, her beast snorted in her mind.

"This is your fault," she muttered, as though the creature would understand.

Ultimately, it didn't matter who was responsible, her dragon's or Declan's. It had happened. This was bound to occur since she was plagued with her cycle. By being denied the protection elixir from the witches, she had to endure heat and called to him. The law of averages meant eventually her mate would answer. And he had. Now what the hell was she supposed to do? How did mating even work?

On one hand, yes, she didn't have to keep going to the mating grounds, hollering her head off. Her dragon couldn't force her to shift because she was horny. But on the other hand, she had this guy bound to her, and she didn't know fuck all about him. He could be just like her father.

He could knock her up and leave her with an egg in favor of another female. Hadn't he mentioned something about lions?

Their bond was so new, and it wasn't solid. It could break easily. Right?

Gods. What had she been taught about *fated* mates? She'd never been around a pair before. Honestly, she thought they were mythical.

She sure made a mess.

Though, had it really been her who made the disaster? Lifting her head, she chewed on her bottom lip as she considered her situation. If the witches hadn't denied helping her mother, she'd still be around. Hell, her father might actually have been in her life. She might have been able to learn how to be a mate for someone. Not to mention Alisa would have had the elixir. She might not even be in Manhattan.

Well, if her father was running his company, yes. She would have been in Manhattan, but it would have been with her family intact. Maybe, in the ideal situation with her mother alive, she would have taken the releaser, and her mating would have been her choice. It wouldn't be thrust upon her so suddenly.

So many what-ifs. They bounced in her mind, giving her a headache. They didn't matter. Her reality was none of those. Any possible happy upbringing had been denied her.

And the Ember Witches were to blame. They did this to her. They robbed her of her mother and deprived Alisa of her father. The witches needed to be held accountable.

Everything else could fall into place once the spellcasters answered for their crimes. Alisa could consider how this whole mating situation could move forward.

The witches first. Then her mate.

Peeling herself off the floor, she took a deep breath. A sense of resolve flowed through her. Even her dragon agreed as the beast nodded in her mind.

Declan

One of the most glorious things about being a dragon shifter was flight. Soaring through the air among the birds had to be the most freeing experience. One day, Declan and his mate would be side by side in the sky. Pure euphoria filled him. He supposed he could attribute his recent mating to the feeling, but there was just something about flying.

Another added bonus was that it made travel so much more efficient. No traffic jams or speed limits occurred in the skies. Sure, the occasional storm and wind could hamper arrival times slightly, but nothing like on land.

Plus, flying with his own wings in his beastly form was a hell of a lot better than going through TSA. There was nothing more annoying than standing in lines, having strangers go through his bags, and taking off his shoes before he could go somewhere.

Yeah, that was definitely his favorite part of being a dragon shifter. Now, he'd be able to enjoy that with a proper mate.

Actually, first he had to learn her name. Referring to her as the golden dragon seemed wrong. She was his mate. He should know her name.

Next time he saw her, he'd definitely ask her. The rutting got in the way the last two occasions, but on the third instance, he'd find out as much as he could about her. Destiny decided she belonged to him and he to her. They needed to explore everything about each other.

In time.

He was getting ahead of himself. He had to slow the fuck down. First, get her to agree they were mates. Second, ask what she liked to be called. Wait. Should he do those in reverse order? Did it matter? Okay, simultaneously. He'd have to do those two together.

21

ALISA

A long, hot shower couldn't wash away the rage burning inside Alisa. While she lathered her shampoo and suds ran over her body, she imagined ways she could exact her revenge against the witches for the hell they put her through and to avenge her mother.

Unfortunately, they weren't exactly well-known. So finding them to give them what the magic bearers deserved would be one hell of a task.

Blowing out a heavy breath, she leaned her head against the wall of her shower. With a balled fist, she tapped the tiles. Someone had to know a witch.

Wait.

She jerked back.

The teal—Declan. Declan was friends with a witch. Her inner dragon snapped her jaws at the thought of the drunken woman beside him the night before. The next female that laid so much as a hair on him would get her head ripped off, for sure.

Shaking that thought away, she willed herself to focus.

Declan was acquainted with a magic bearer. While not all witches were Ember Witches, the ones responsible for her mother's death, and her own personal Hades, were. To her knowledge, the spellcaster world was tight-knit. Logically, that meant his magic-bearing friend had to be familiar with someone who might have met an Ember Witch. Her dragon grumbled at the thought of relying on the tiara-wearing magic bearer for anything. It was a start. It was the only lead she had.

Speaking of beginnings. She needed to haul her ass into bed so she could head to Fever early and commence groveling to keep her job. Ditching mid-shift wasn't exactly excusable. Sure, Jason was a shifter and was familiar with general quirks, but *this* was a bit extreme. Not to mention it was on one of their busiest nights. Yeah, she was fucked.

It would take some sincere begging if she planned on staying at the only place in the city that would actually understand her plight. Maybe discovering her mate wasn't entirely bad. If she told Jason her heat would no longer cause her to bail unexpectedly, he might be more inclined to allow her to keep her job.

Reluctantly, Alisa turned the knob, and the flow of the water ceased. It'd been the ideal temperature. She could've been under the spray in there for hours, but she had shit to do—a mother to avenge and witches to decimate.

How she wished, for the first time in her life, that she was a male fire dragon. Were she a dude, stumbling upon her destined other half would've given her the ability to breathe fire. That would make destroying Ember Witches a hell of a lot easier. She'd have to fight them a different way.

In time, she would figure that shit out. For now, she needed to crawl into bed and take a nap or else she'd be useless when she went to the night club.

If Jason let her back in Fever.

Optimism had to be her ally. She had enough negativity swirling around her.

Once she slid on a pair of panties and a tank top, she toppled onto her bed. Crawling up toward the pillows, she tried to create a comfortable nest for the best sleep. After she flicked the switch for her fan to blow cool air on her while she slept, she grabbed her sleep mask.

If nothing else, she needed a good day's rest.

Kaboom!

"What the fuck?" Shooting straight up from her cozy spot, Alisa ripped off her mask and charged toward the sound.

As she reached for the knob to her bedroom door, a force punched her in the gut. With the wind knocked out of her lungs and her limbs flailed out, Alisa flew back, colliding with her bed.

Splinters of door rained down around her as hurricane-force winds swirled through the room. Gasping, trying to catch her breath, she frantically scanned around. What or who had just launched an assault on her?

The beast within her roared and slammed against her mental confines for release. She wanted to fight whatever had just entered their apartment. However, that wasn't feasible. There wasn't enough space. She'd destroy it even more if she set her dragon free.

As her dirty clothes, shoes, backpack, lotions, and everything else she owned whirled around her, Alisa, with her heart racing, finally got a good view of the culprit.

A woman, who appeared to be in her mid-fifties from the creases around her eyes and the strands of gray hairs woven into her medium-brown loose plait, had literally burst into her apartment entirely unannounced—and was quite unwelcome. While it took everything Alisa had to not fly off into the windstorm, the woman seemed unaffected by the surrounding commotion. Her long, loose-fitting beige cotton dress didn't so much as flutter.

She glared at Alisa with a rage burning in her eyes Alisa had never seen before.

What had she done to spark this woman's ire? Who the hell was she?

"Did you think *we* wouldn't *know* you had arrived?" the woman demanded.

Who the fuck was *we*? Alisa blinked up at her, filled with confusion.

"You were supposed to stay in the mountains. *Exiled*."

"By whom?" But Alisa put two and two together, and fire boiled in her veins. Her dragon roared, desperate to attack. But she just couldn't let it.

Just as Alisa went to stand, the woman's arms shot forward, and another blast of air pummeled Alisa, pinning her against her bed in a seated position.

"You're *cursed*. Golden dragons deserve no peace for what they've done."

"Screw you!" Alisa spat.

The woman flicked her wrist, and one of Alisa's Converse sneakers slapped her in the face so hard it snapped her head to the side. Pain blossomed on her cheek, and ire blazed in her chest. Balling her hands into fists, she gritted her teeth, trying to stand against the wind holding her in place.

"The sins of the mother are passed down. You cannot escape it. Consider this your only warning to leave. You do not want to face the full wrath of the Ember Witches upon you."

"I didn't do anything."

"You're golden. It is your birthright to shoulder this burden. Never to mate. Your line to die out. The history of your kind has proven detrimental to all."

"Fuck off! That's not fair!"

"The fates care not of such things."

"This has nothing to do with them!" Alisa screeched. It couldn't be. Destiny had just dealt her a mate. Why would they want her to suffer endlessly? "This is petty witch revenge."

The woman's eye twitched. "I caution you one final time. Go away. Retreat to the mountains where you belong. Suffer your misfortune with dignity and know it is the right path for all of us. Do not interpret my leniency for weakness."

With a snap of her fingers, she vanished. The wind stopped. Things which had broken were repaired. Items out of place were back in their spots—like nothing had happened.

The pressure holding Alisa still evaporated.

It was as though the witch had never even been there—like Alisa had dreamed it.

But it wasn't her imagination. She'd stood in her apartment. The threat was clear.

Alisa just didn't understand it.

History of her kind? What did that even mean? All she'd been told about was her mother's transgression. Yes, if her father was to be believed, it was beyond egregious. But one dragon did not constitute history.

There had to be more to the story.

Pushing herself to her feet, Alisa glanced around her room. There was only one person who knew golden dragon history—the only other golden dragon. Her grandmother.

Perhaps a trip back to the mountains was overdue.

22

DECLAN

Normally, heat didn't bother Declan. As an ice dragon shifter, he could essentially self-cool. His blood ran colder than most. So swiping beads of sweat off his brow was a new experience for him. Staring at his moist fingers, he was quite perplexed.

Glancing around, he took in the tall palm trees, the sand beneath his feet, and the large entrance of a cavern in a mountainside. Lush greenery covered the slopes, but at the peak, he spotted smoke.

The smell of burning and ash filled his nostrils.

Cocking his head to the side, he considered the possibilities.

Obviously, a volcano. He stood at the base of a volcano among ferns and coconut trees. How the hell had he gotten there?

When the ground shook, he glanced skyward. It wasn't anything a human could have detected. The wind shifted, and he anticipated darker plumes. Taking a deep breath, he expected bright molten lava to shoot from the top.

Except, nothing had changed.

Curious.

Furrowing his brow, he lowered his eyes and considered other possibilities.

Perhaps it was just a tiny earthquake and the only reason he even detected it was because he was a shifter and had enhanced senses. Nodding, he decided to be satisfied with that conclusion.

He wasn't. Something nagged at him. But a quake was the only logical assumption.

Several twigs snapped in the distance. Turning toward the sound, he narrowed his eyes and braced himself, preparing to react to whatever had done it. This tropical environment could be home to many things—jaguars, elephants. Who knew what called the surrounding jungle home.

While not exactly pounding, his heart rate increased as anticipation built. The leaves of the ferns beside him rustled, and his muscles tightened. He curled his fingers and made fists, preparing to defend himself against whatever would emerge.

The grains of sand beneath his feet vibrated. This wasn't a quake. Something large headed toward him.

No fucking way.

With wide eyes, his hands fell limp at his sides. His mouth hung open as he stared in wonder.

Grumbling as he moseyed out from the thick brush was a massive teal dragon. Stunned, he blinked his blue eyes repeatedly. Declan couldn't believe what he saw before him. His long thick neck swayed with each one of his lazy clawed steps toward the mouth of the cave in the volcano. This couldn't be real. His wings were tucked low on his back so he could fit through the entranceway. As his tail dragged behind him, Declan was tempted to reach out to touch it.

How was this even possible? They existed together. There was no way they could be separate. His dragon couldn't be its own distinct creature. That wasn't how any of this worked.

"Declan?" His mother's voice startled him.

On a gasp, he jolted awake. Breathing heavily, he gripped the blanket tighter. Allowing his eyes a moment to focus, he realized he'd fallen asleep on the couch in parents' living room after he'd thrown some sweatpants on.

"You okay?" she asked as she lowered herself to the sturdy coffee table.

Declan scrubbed his face as he sat up. "Just an interesting dream."

Sitting back, his mother peered at him with a suspicious expression. She crossed her arms and pursed her lips while studying him.

"What?" He glanced around, shifting uncomfortably under her intense stare. It wasn't like he had a hard-on. "Why are you looking at me like that?"

"You're different."

He furrowed his brows. "Huh? How?"

She leaned forward and inhaled. With a smirk, she clucked her tongue. "Eli," she called over her shoulder. "Come in here."

"What?" Declan repeated as he and his dragon's annoyance rose.

His father entered, wearing loose-fitting flannel pants and carrying two mugs with steam coming off them.

"Yeah. Oh!" A smile spread across his face. "Declan. I didn't know you were here. Good to see you."

Declan's dad continued deeper into the room and offered a beverage to his mom. "To what do we owe this pleasant surprise?"

"You can't tell?" his mother scoffed.

Sipping what Declan could only assume to be hot chocolate by the smell, his father lifted his shoulders.

She rolled her eyes and sighed. "Typical. Males aren't as sensitive as we are."

"Hey," his father rebuked.

"I'm just saying. You should be able to pick up on it."

"On what?" Declan slapped his hands on the cushions of the couch, incensed his mother wouldn't just come out and say it.

"You don't smell it?" His mother gestured to Declan.

"Do I stink or something?" He lifted his arm and tried to sniff his own armpit. He'd showered the day before.

She chuckled.

His father leaned in and inhaled deeply. "I dunno. I mean, I guess there's a little different scent. But he flew here, so I don't want to make assumptions. He could've tangled with something on the way. That's none of my business."

Exasperated, his mother huffed. "So, who's the lucky female?" She refocused her attention on Declan.

Stuttering slightly, he took a moment to realize what she meant. His brows lifted in surprise, and he couldn't help but grin. His inner dragon grumped but otherwise curled himself into a ball so he could rest.

"Honestly, I don't have a clue." He scrubbed the back of his neck as he lowered his head, slightly ashamed he hadn't asked the golden dragon her name yet.

"What female?" his father asked cluelessly.

"Seriously?" His mother slapped her husband's thigh beside her. "Your son is mated."

"Oh!" His father raised his mug. "Congratulations."

"Yeah," Declan said on a sigh. "Thanks." Frowning, he met his mother's beaming gaze.

"Tell us about her," she said before sipping at her cocoa.

"I wish I could." Declan fell back onto the couch. "We met at the mating grounds."

"Oh! A dragon!" his dad interrupted excitedly.

"How fortunate," his mom chimed in.

"Yeah, yeah," Declan said dismissively. "All I know is she's golden and has an apartment in the city."

"Wait, if you're mated, why are you here?" his father asked.

His mother cocked her head to the side but kept silent. Her gaze beckoned him to explain.

Shifting on the couch, he tried to escape the discomfort of having had her walk out on him twice. "I don't think she's ready for our mating. Like it must have been her first time at the mating grounds or something."

His mom's brows knit together. "What do you mean?"

"After we rutted, she took off," Declan explained. "Both times."

"So, she called you to the mating grounds and ditched you after?" his father repeated.

"Well, the second occasion we didn't go to the mating grounds."

"It doesn't always happen at the mating grounds," his mother offered. "It can happen anywhere, but we sows are drawn to Ireland."

His father nodded. "Okay."

"But why did she leave?" his mother asked.

Declan shrugged. "She hasn't exactly been communicating much. She hasn't even told me her name yet. I mean, we will get there, but I want to give her space so she can sort out whatever is holding her back. It's not like she can escape me. We're mates. Fate won't let us be apart."

His mother hummed as she sipped her cocoa.

"Well, don't stay separate for too long," his father warned. "If you do, the mate dreams are gonna be a bitch."

"What are those?" Declan asked.

"Yeah, if you're with your mate enough, you can avoid them. Your dragon will be content with the real-life interaction. But when you're apart, the beast longs for its mate.

And since the animal isn't usually in full control of the body, he commands what he can," his father explained.

Declan peered at his parents in confusion. This was new information. No one talked about mate dreams when he was a kid.

His mother reached forward and patted his knee, drawing his focus toward her. "Mated shifters establish a bond."

"Yeah." Declan nodded. He knew that much.

"Well, their dragons, or whatever their animals are, form a deeper bond and connect in such a way where they can invite their other half to their den or lair."

"Huh?" This made no sense. "My dragon doesn't have a den."

"Of course he does. It's just inside your consciousness. It's where he lives when you're walking about in your human form. Where do you think he goes?" his father scoffed.

Declan opened his mouth, but no words came out. Really? A mental lair? "I never really thought about it before. I mean, when he's out to play, I just kind of descend into darkness."

"Well, you're in human form more than you're in dragon. So, you just haven't had enough time to establish a place," his father suggested.

"Fair point." Declan rubbed his chin as he considered all they'd just told him.

"Anyway," his dad continued. "The more you're apart, the more, uh, intense those dreamland den visits become. It contributes to the madness shifters can experience if they are separated from their mates for too long."

"Well, I don't plan on being away for more than a few days," Declan asserted.

His mother grinned. "That's my boy."

Now all he had to do was figure out how to convince his mate to hang out with him so they didn't descend into insanity at the hands of their inner dragons.

23

ALISA

Shifting back and forth from human to dragon, then flying took a lot of energy. Even for a shifter who had preternatural healing abilities. It was draining. Alisa stumbled as she made her way to the small shed in the yard of her grandmother's home. Inside, there was a couch and a dresser filled with clothing.

Humans, prudish as they were, frowned upon showing up nude anywhere. Especially in the US. She might get away with it in Europe.

When her shifts came on faster than she could plan for them, she lost outfits. So she needed a safe place to return to where she could be naked with no one catching her. Thankfully, the mountains weren't all that far.

The acreage of land her grandmother owned was surrounded by forest. So, if anyone saw her without clothes on the property, they had to go out of their way to do so. Also, the nearest neighbor was about five miles down the road.

"Lee?" her grandmother called from the expansive deck in the back of the house after Alisa exited the shed, dressed in leggings and a tank top. "What are you doing here?"

Trudging through the yard, Alisa wasn't sure if she had the oomph to truly get into it, but she had to say something.

"Lee." Her grandmother's tone shifted to one laced with concern. Rising to her feet, she eyed Alisa warily.

"We need to talk." Alisa flopped into a cushioned chair on the deck. She hoped she could stay awake through this conversation.

Her grandmother's gaze went from her head to her feet and back up again. Her lips tightened into a line. She took a deep inhale before she sat back slowly in her own chair. "I feel like I should congratulate you, but you don't look happy."

Alisa was far too exhausted to play games, so she cut to the chase. "Are golden dragons cursed?"

With pursed lips, her grandmother glanced away.

"I know I am. But I mean more than that. Like before I was ever hatched. Are you cursed? Was my mother cursed? Who did it and why?"

No answer. Her grandmother seemed fixated on something far off in the distance. Something about her expression and her eyes hinted she was lost in a memory.

"Grandma." Alisa tried to bring her back to the present. "What is the curse?"

Licking her lips, her grandmother shifted in her chair. Her attention fell to the ground. "It's been said for generations golden dragons were the first to lose their fate-chosen mates. We had to select our mates. Our males died out long ago."

"That makes no sense. Fate can give us any kind of mate." Alisa shook her head. "If we can hatch baby golden dragons, why can't they be male?"

"I'm sure someone smarter than me can link it to some sort of genetic marker or something scientific like that, but what happened was an Ember Witch and a golden dragon fell for the same male. When he chose the dragon, the witch didn't handle it well and cursed them never to have male dragons, only female, and that is how the males died off. Which made it harder for our kind to find our fated mates because they didn't exist. And if we chose a mate, he took on our curse and was not long for this world. They call it the sin of the mother. I had hoped if I kept you in the mountains, it would be safer."

That last bit sounded familiar. The Ember Witch in her apartment had said the same.

"But we don't have to mate with golden dragons. We can bond with anything. Fate decides," Alisa reiterated. There had to be more.

Her grandmother drew in another deep breath. "I suppose." She lifted her gaze to meet Alisa's. "You seem to have done just that. You're connected. I can smell him on you. That is, unless you have established a chosen mate in the short time you've been gone."

Alisa covered her shoulder where Declan had marked her. "Fate seems to have given me a mate, but an Ember Witch says it can't be."

Her grandmother stiffened, and her eyes widened. "An Ember Witch found you?"

"Apparently."

"They never liked golden dragons. Your mother only made it worse. She tried to fight against the curse." Somberly, her grandmother's voice trailed off.

Covering her face with her hands, Alisa rubbed up and down. "So, what my father said about my mother is true? She destroyed an egg and went after witches?"

Anger flared in her grandmother's eyes, and smoke came from her nostrils. Her jaw tightened. "Your father did not honor his chosen mate. Your mother suffered from unrequited mating. She cannot be blamed for what your father did."

Stunned, Alisa couldn't believe it was all true. "*He* didn't kill an unborn dragon."

"I pray you never experience the misery of a half mating. Even chosen mates can experience the pain of separation. The pain is like no hell you can ever imagine. It brings on madness. We cannot be held responsible for what we do in that state." Her grandmother sounded as though she was pleading. "The Ember Witches are to blame for this."

"Some actions are inexcusable." Alisa's world had turned on its axis. It was too much. Her mother was a murderer. Alisa was cursed. The Ember Witches, the most powerful coven in the world, despised her existence. Gods. Could it get any worse?

"Like cursing an entire species of dragon, I agree." Her grandmother jutted her head in a nod before reaching for Alisa's hand. "But you've *broken* it. You didn't choose him, you were given him, and you're mated. Now you have to protect him."

"What?" Hold the phone. She had to do what now?

"When they find out, they *will* come for him. They *will* rip him from you like they did your father from your mother and your grandfather from me." Urgency gripped her words. She squeezed Alisa's hands. "You can have what we've all been denied. Fate may have forgiven you, us, but the Ember Witches are petty bitter bitches."

Of course, they were. She'd already figured out the Ember Witches were evil. They killed her mom, but then again, her mom had done some seriously heinous shit.

But could she really be blamed if she was carrying the burden of a curse the same fucking witches bestowed upon her? Could she have actually had her chosen mate if the witches hadn't gotten involved? It could've been avoided had the witches not cursed them.

The world would never know, but one thing was for sure, the Ember Witches needed to go down.

But how the hell was Alisa supposed to do that? With her eyelids drooping, she couldn't focus anymore. She'd have to figure everything out tomorrow.

24

ALISA

Shivering, Alisa wrapped her arms around herself in an attempt to get warm. As a fire dragon, she never—ever—got cold. She had a flame inside her that burned to keep her heated like a furnace. Even in the heaviest of snows, she could frolic completely nude and not feel any sort of chill.

Except right now.

What the hell was going on? Where the fuck was she?

While standing ankle-deep in snow, she glanced around. She took in the massive drifts to her left and right with evergreens weighed down with icicles and snow circling her. An enormous shale mountain capped with ice was several yards in front of her.

Was this Siberia? Alaska, maybe.

Eeeeeee. Her breath caught in her throat. With wide eyes, she spun around and searched the vast forest behind her for the source of the screech.

Eeeeeee. It was familiar, but she couldn't place it.

Rawr. *Again, she whirled, almost dizzy. With a hand on her head, trying to stabilize herself, Alisa gaped at the teal dragon standing at the mouth of the cave. He was such a magnificent creature. His scales glistened as the snowflakes fell on them. With his long neck arched, he bellowed again.* Rawr.

Who did he summon?

Eeeeeee. There it was again. She knew that call.

Peeking over her shoulder, she stumbled. Brows raised, she couldn't believe what she saw. No fucking way. It couldn't be possible.

She patted her chest as though to check herself.

After snapping branches, a golden dragon emerged from the wintery wood with her wings resting on her back and smoke coming from her nostrils. She may have never seen her reflection, but she'd know that beast anywhere.

It was her dragon.

How had it separated itself?

Stomping past Alisa like she didn't exist, her golden dragon swished her long tail slightly as she approached the teal dragon at the cave entrance.

Stumbling back, so as not to get accidentally hit with the tip of the tail, Alisa rested against the rough trunk of a tree.

This made no sense. They were dual beings. Their existence depended on each other. They just couldn't appear this way. It wasn't possible to be separate.

Her head spun.

The dragons, unfazed by her presence, nuzzled against one another. Their affection warmed her against the cold but made her heart ache. Placing her hand on her chest, as though that would somehow soothe her, one name came to mind.

A longing blossomed within her. Their dragons were together, but their humans weren't. It felt like a barbed wire coiled around her heart, tightening and constricting. Her knees wobbled.

As the two dragons continued their canoodling, a need took root.

She wanted him.

Declan.

On a gasp, Alisa jolted and nearly fell out of the deck chair. Clutching a blanket she had no idea how she obtained to her chest, she panted and held on to the arm of her seat. Surveying her surroundings, she realized it was warm out. Not a single snow crystal in sight. Though trees were aplenty, she noticed she'd lost daylight.

Her grandmother's yard. Okay, that made sense. Closing her eyes, she internally searched for her dragon. Her shoulders relaxed when she found her beast curled up inside her mind, resting.

Whew. They were together again. It was just a dream.

How long had she been asleep?

"You're finally awake," her grandmother commented as she slid the glass door open and joined her on the deck.

"Yeah." Alisa sat back in the chair to get herself comfortable again.

Except a sense of unease had settled in her gut. Her chest hurt in a way it never had before. It wasn't from an injury. It was something else.

"You missed the entire day." Her grandmother chuckled. "Must have been one hell of a morning," she said, wearing a smirk.

Shaking it off, Alisa extended her hand. "Can I use your phone?"

Her grandmother regarded her warily.

Alisa raised her brows to emphasize her request. "I left mine at the bar. My shift came on too fast. I need to check my messages."

When had her grandmother ever second-guessed her?

Hesitantly, her grandma reached into the pocket of her housecoat. Slowly, she offered her cell to Alisa.

Practically snatching it out of her hand, Alisa dismissed her suspicion. After dialing her own number, she followed the prompts and entered her code to check her voicemail.

"You have two new voice messages," said the robotic lady.

Alisa tapped the screen to play the first message. Her grandmother crossed her arms and sat back with her gaze fixated on Alisa.

It made Alisa shift in her seat. What was that about? She had never seen her grandma so suspicious of her. For a moment, she considered listening to the messages in private, but she suspected the voicemail to be Jason checking in on her. She had just abandoned him. Maybe he wasn't following up with her. He might fire her.

"Alisa, it's Jason. We need to talk. Call me." Yep. Exactly what she thought.

She tapped to delete the message and played the second one. Her boss sounded pissed. If he left her a second message, she was definitely fired for sure.

"Hi. Alisa? It's Duncan Hayes." Her spine went rigid.

Her gaze flicked toward her grandmother, who had leaned in and narrowed her eyes.

Alisa definitely should have gone out of earshot for this. Too late now.

"I wanted to let you know the offer for dinner still stands, but I understand if that would be too much."

How the hell did he get her number in the first place? She never gave it to him.

"How about we do lunch? Every afternoon, I eat at a café on the corner of my building. If you're open to meeting so we can chat, I will be there. If not, it's okay. No pressure. I understand our last meeting gave you a lot to process, and I'd like to help with that if I can."

Alisa deleted the message and took a deep breath. There was too much happening all at once. The truth about her mother was hard enough to swallow but add on a mate, an additional curse, witches threatening her, and now her dad actually wanting a relationship. This was way more than she bargained for.

"Do you have your boss's number? You need to call him and tell him you aren't returning."

"What?" Alisa gaped, unsure she heard her grandmother correctly. Inside the confines of her mind, her dragon perked.

"You can't go back there. If the Ember Witches find you again, they won't be so kind. We can replace whatever you have in the apartment."

She couldn't be serious.

"And your mate, he will find you in the mountains. He located you once. He can do it again."

Her inner beast scoffed at the idea of being separated from her mate any longer than she already had been.

"This isn't your decision." Her inner dragon nodded her approval of Alisa's stance.

"Excuse me?"

"I'm not going to let some old-ass bitch tell me where I can be."

"She's not just—"

"I'm a golden dragon. I go where I want." Alisa lifted her chin and rolled her shoulders back. She wasn't about to let anyone tell her what to do. Ember Witch or not, there was too much in Manhattan she needed to settle.

Not to mention, by going there, she could flush out this Ember Witch and give her what was coming to her. They might be a powerful coven, but their vendetta had gone far enough. They couldn't keep punishing her family for something that wasn't their fault.

"Lee, you have to listen. Your mother thought she could take them on too." Her grandmother reached for her hands and held them tight. "I cannot lose you too. You should be smart about this."

"I will not hide from them. This has gone on far too long. They cannot continue to deny golden dragons their fates."

Her grandmother tightened her lips into a thin line. "You don't understand who they are."

"I know *full well* who they are and what I am up against, but if I don't fight for us, who will?" Her mind raced with ideas on how she might fight off an Ember Witch, let alone an entire coven. It was definitely going to be nearly impossible, but someone had to.

Shaking her head, her grandma waved a hand as though to brush the idea away. "No. I will not allow you to do that."

Alisa scoffed. "You don't have a choice."

"You will not battle with them."

"If you don't support me, I will get someone else to." Alisa slammed the cell phone down on the table and stood.

"Who?" Her grandmother demanded as she rose.

"My family," Alisa sneered.

Flames danced behind her grandmother's eyes. "You will not see that man again. I forbid it. He is just as cursed as the rest of us and will only make it worse. He probably led the witch right to you."

Having said everything she needed to, Alisa turned. With clenched fists and a tight jaw, she marched down the stairs of the deck and into the yard. She stripped, tossing her clothes aside. This had gone on long enough. There was no sense in waiting.

Closing her eyes, she summoned her dragon. The beast was more than prepared to come forth, and it was probably the quickest and least painful shift of her life.

"Alisa!" her grandmother hollered.

Without looking back, Alisa, in dragon form, snatched the clothing in her claws before she took off and headed to the island of Manhattan. She would put an end to the curse of the golden dragons one way or another.

25

DECLAN

After a long shower, Declan sat on the edge of the bed in his parents' guest room wearing boxer briefs and smearing lotion on his body. His dragon had scales, but his human didn't have to be ashy.

When his finger grazed over the raised scar of his mating mark, his dragon huffed in frustration. Knots tightened in his stomach, and his chest ached. They'd been separated for mere hours, and he was already uncomfortable. The mate dream was odd, and he would apparently experience more with higher intensity the longer they kept their distance from each other.

Hanging his head, he put the bottle of lotion back on the end table. Without a plan, he'd never convince his mate it was a good idea to be together. Which, honestly, she *should* know. He flopped on the bed and let his arms flail out. How was he supposed to do this before their separation drove them both insane?

As a shifter herself, she had to be aware of the consequences of denying their destiny. Yet she still fled. Something had to have spooked her away from their fate. But what? Could it be as simple as inexperience?

He'd never been in a serious relationship before. Everything he'd done in the past had been casual flings with consenting adults—shifters and otherwise. But this was different. This was his *mate.* Fate selected her just for him. It should be easier. Shouldn't it?

Then again, did mates date? Was he supposed to wine and dine her? That was what humans did, not shifters. Okay, he'd admit Gideon had to do that with Ella, but they had different circumstances. Declan's female *should* understand how things went.

However, it seemed his sow understood little. If she had, she wouldn't have run from him. *Twice.*

Was she playing hard to get?

No. He flipped his hand through the air as though to swat away the idea. Shifters didn't play those sorts of human games. Instincts drove their kind. They were closer to their animals in that sense.

Or… they were supposed to be.

Godsdammit. Why was his mate such an enigma? What was she thinking? There had to be more to the story.

Letting out a heavy breath, he rolled onto his stomach and reached for a phone. He didn't know how women thought. So, he'd have to call in reinforcements.

Dialing her number quickly from his parents' landline, he waited for the rings, and of course, she didn't answer. Why would she? This was a strange number. No one took calls from unknown callers anymore.

"Hey, it's me. I'm at my parents', but I need your advice. I'm gonna swing by your place later. Be home." He placed the phone on its cradle and rolled onto his back again.

He should've learned from Gideon's mating. Fate could be a downright bitch. First, it handed Gideon someone he didn't think would give him his fire. Now, it dealt Declan a partner who didn't appear to want to be bonded but took the releaser to find him.

It made little sense. He needed a female's perspective. It'd be the only way he could understand and right this ship. Obviously, he'd missed something.

A shifter would be a better option, but all the female shifters he knew were hookups. It felt like bad form to go to them with questions about his mate. He never really established a friendship with them.

This wasn't the type of situation he could discuss with his mother, and his sisters were busy with their own shit. Maybe his sisters could help. Except Scarlett was recently mated, and he didn't want to interrupt their rutting. Tessa was merely twenty-three. She hadn't even taken the releaser yet. She couldn't assist.

Nodding to himself, he knew his choice was solid. Felicity would give him good advice. She was his last hope. Unfortunately, that meant his trip home would be short.

With a groan, he pushed off the bed and headed out of the room. After he answered some emails for work, he could focus on getting support with solving his mate's problem. No need to wait on this. The sooner he sorted it out, the better.

The night before, Declan showed up at Felicity's place with Mexican food. This time, he had to bring a better peace offering for abandoning her when they were supposed to celebrate her birthday.

One could argue there was nothing better than tacos. Glancing down at the bags in his hands, doubt settled in. Had he made the right choice? What was her favorite food? Ah, hell if he knew. They didn't talk about shit like that.

Come to think of it, it would be nice to find out what his mate preferred. He added that to the list of stuff he wanted to learn about her. Did she enjoy salty or sweet? Declan was partial to salty.

Focus.

He'd never get answers about what his mate liked or didn't if he couldn't get her to talk to him. Hell, he'd settle for her sticking around for longer than a few minutes after rutting. It would be nice to learn more about the female fate chose for him.

Felicity would know what to do. She had to. He had no other ideas.

Taking a deep breath, he rolled his shoulders back and held his head high. Shifting the bags from one in each hand to hold them together, he raised his fist and rapped on his friend's door.

He hadn't heard from her, but she worked from home most of the time. So, the odds were in his favor she'd be there.

"Declan!" With her hair in a haphazard bun atop her head and wearing sweatpants and a tank top, she definitely wasn't expecting company. Obviously caught off guard to see him, she fidgeted, shifting her weight from foot to foot while fussing with her messy bun and glancing around nervously.

Oh, well. He was on a mission. Lifting the bags, he grinned. "I brought sushi." Sheepishly, he hung his head. "It's my apology for ditching you."

"Who's there?" a voice from behind Felicity called.

The dragon within Declan stiffened within his mind.

Drawing his brows together, Declan lowered the sacks of food and peered first at his friend and then past her. "I'm sorry, am I interrupting?"

It'd been a woman. So why did his hackles raise and his dragon go on high alert?

Felicity glanced over her shoulder briefly before facing him again and closing the door slightly yet leaning on it. She seemed to be hiding something. He couldn't be sure if it was him from her visitor or the other way around.

"This is a bad time," she whispered.

Definitely keeping him from her guest. But why?

His dragon sat up on his haunches inside the confines of Declan's mind. What had him so wary? Could it be the way Felicity acted or the other person's tone? Declan didn't recognize it. How could his beast?

Wait!

Did she think he'd care if she took someone home after he left the bar? He grinned at the thought.

"Are you with someone?" he whispered playfully, amused she might be embarrassed by a one-night stand.

"Uh." Again, she glanced behind her before returning her focus to him with anxiety radiating off her.

Definitely a hookup.

"Kind of, but not like that." She chewed on her bottom lip.

She was essentially his only female friend. They weren't lovers by any stretch of the imagination. So, there was no reason for her to be awkward about taking someone home. What else could it be?

"Are you doing an interview?" he asked.

While she'd never invited her work to her home before, it didn't mean this couldn't be the first time.

Shuffling behind Felicity drew his and his beast's attention. His dragon snarled in his mind. Something wasn't right.

Shifting her gaze away from him, she shook her head. "I just. I—"

The door swung open. Declan bent his knees, dropped the food, and raised his hands—on guard. Beside Felicity stood an older woman. Her wavy brown hair had streaks of gray, and it hung loose down past her shoulders. Crow's feet spider-webbed out from the corners of her eyes as she narrowed them at him. An aura glowed around her.

Based on looks alone, she appeared to be some older woman, but there was more to her. An energy radiated off her. A witch. That's what had his dragon in a tizzy.

She held magic inside her. Declan and his dragon could feel it. For some reason, it made his beast nervous.

"You're not the golden dragon." She leaned out of the apartment and glanced around.

"Uh, no." He regarded her skeptically. Who the hell was she, and how did she know about Declan's mate?

Pulling back, the woman glared at him. "Stay away from her. She will give you the curse."

"Auntie!" Felicity admonished.

Curse? Had he heard correctly? "Like a hex?" he blurted.

The older woman stepped back. "Come in." She waved at him.

"I'm sorry." Felicity sounded tired. "This is my aunt Josephine. Please forgive her. She can be *rude* when she's carrying out her duties."

Perplexed, Declan retrieved the food and entered the apartment. While there was plenty of energy swirling in the air, he wasn't sure if it was Felicity or her aunt—hell, it could be both. It was way more potent than normal. Declan's inner dragon hissed as they passed the woman.

So, the aunt was a witch. But why was his beast reacting that way? He'd been around Felicity for months now, and he didn't care about her magical tendencies.

Shit. Hold up.

"Are you an Ember Witch?" he asked as he placed the sushi on the counter in the small kitchen area of the apartment.

A slight smirk spread on the older woman's face as she dipped her chin in acknowledgement.

"No shit. Are you the one—wait." He shifted his focus to Felicity. "Is she the one who threw Ella off the mountain?"

Now it made sense. Of course, his dragon reacted negatively toward the older witch. He stood in solidarity with his friend.

"It was necessary for them to accept their mating," Felicity's aunt declared firmly.

"I dunno. Seemed a little extreme when a simple talk could have done the trick," he muttered as he unpacked the food.

"They were beyond a conversation. There are times fate demands unorthodox measures to get the point across." Her words were sharp.

His dragon snapped his jaws.

That was more than loyalty to his friend.

"The two of you"—she waved a finger between them—"need to keep away from the golden dragon. They bring only pain and suffering to those around them. Especially witches."

The hairs on the back of his neck rose. His beast growled. Declan's lip curled in a snarl. She spoke ill of his mate. That could not be tolerated.

The older woman arched a brow at him. "It's for your own safety. Felicity's parents went against us and befriended a golden dragon, and look at what happened to them. I will *not* stand by and see her suffer the same fate."

There was so much coming at him at once. Declan blinked, trying to process it. "Your parents? They're—"

"My biological parents. My adoptive parents are fine," Felicity clarified. "You have to excuse Auntie Josephine. She can be quite dramatic. I told her the only dragons I know are you and Gideon."

"But you..." Felicity's aunt pointed an accusatory finger at Declan.

His beast lowered his chest, preparing to pounce, and it was all Declan could do to prevent his human half from doing the same. Instead, he narrowed his eyes at her.

Yep. He definitely didn't like Felicity's aunt.

Felicity cleared her throat. "Anyway, as I was saying, neither one of you is gold. Not that I've seen you as dragons, but from what I'm told, golden ones only come in female. And since Ella is human, and you're single, there are no other dragons around." She shrugged dismissively with an air of annoyance as she turned her attention to the older witch.

"And what's wrong with golden ones?" he asked, sitting on a stool while his inner animal thrashed inside him.

"They're cursed." Josephine sneered.

Nodding, he pressed. "Yeah, I got that, but what does that mean? Who did it and why?"

"*We* did." Felicity's aunt lifted her chin and puffed out her chest as though in pride. "One murdered Felicity's parents after trying to steal the mate of another. Their matings lead to suffering. They cannot be trusted. You must stay away from them."

A bowling ball slammed into his gut and shoved all the air from his lungs. But his dragon, no, he was on the offense. He clawed at the barriers. The beast wanted out to defend the good name—which he didn't know—of their mate.

"They need to be wiped out for the good of all." Josephine folded her arms and glared at him again. "Especially to protect those they attempt to claim as their mates. Fate has always come to collect their chosen mates. So, it is never safe to befriend or even be near a golden dragon. There are only two left. Our job is almost done."

He couldn't hold back the snarl. His dragon barreled into his mental prison. Declan visibly flinched.

"That seems a bit much," Felicity interjected. "Have the two remaining golden dragons done anything yet?"

"They will if we let them. It's inevitable."

26

ALISA

Back in Manhattan, fully clothed, Alisa's first stop was Fever. Unsure of what she would actually *say* to Jason, she needed to go there to, at least, get her phone. The place wouldn't be open for business, but her boss would be on-site. Between deliveries, general maintenance, and the paperwork that had to be done to run a club, he'd be behind his desk.

It was all fun and games at night with the lights down low, the music blasting, and fog machines blowing smoke around drunken young people. It was completely different during the day. The multicolored, light-up dance floor seemed dull without power to it. The space seemed gigantic when all the gyrating bodies had left.

Climbing the stairs, she wished she had called him before arriving, but she hadn't memorized his number. Also, she didn't have her phone.

Once at his office, she gently knocked on the crow shifter's door. Clasping and re-clasping her hands, she shifted her weight from foot to foot. She had no idea why she was nervous. It would go one of two ways. Did it even matter? She hadn't even decided how much longer she'd be in Manhattan.

"Come in, Alisa," he called.

He was a shifter. Of course, he knew it was her.

Rolling her shoulders back with her head high, she twisted the knob, opened the door, and entered the small office.

Jason, a short spindly-looking man wearing round black wire-rimmed glasses, bent over a desk strewn with papers. Without making eye contact, he pushed a cell phone toward the front of the desk.

Closing the door behind her, Alisa entered the room. Swallowing hard, she took a seat and reached for her phone.

"Thank you," she said, tucking it into her pocket.

"I'm quite lenient," he began, keeping his attention on the forms he reviewed. "As a shifter myself, I do understand sometimes we are not in control of ourselves."

Her lips thinned into a hard line and nodded, still trying to sort out what she actually wanted from this meeting other than her phone.

"So, I'm willing to listen. Why did you walk out on your shift during our busiest night of the week?" he asked as he placed the pen down and met her gaze with a blank expression.

Well, fuck.

She inhaled and took a deep, audible breath.

How much could she actually share with him? Hell, he probably didn't want to hear half of what she had to say. Her problems weren't his.

But he asked, so she owed him some sort of explanation.

Keep it simple.

"My dragon is having a difficult time, and some personal stuff has really hit the fan lately. I can't apologize enough for leaving you high and dry so abruptly. I wish I hadn't. Believe me. If I could go back in time, there is a lot I would do differently. That said, I understand if my"—she paused, searching for the correct word—"situation is too unreliable."

His chair creaked when he reclined and interlaced his fingers over his stomach. He pursed his lips as he studied her.

She did her best not to squirm under his scrutiny.

The silence ate at her while the clock on the wall ticked so loud it made her want to rip it from the wall.

Her boss steepled his fingers and tapped them against his chin. "I've employed many a shifter. Until you applied, I was confident I'd encountered one of every type. Then you, a dragon, showed up." He grinned. "I thought I was familiar with every quirk shifters can present with. It's actually been quite fascinating learning so much about all the different varieties." He paused on a deep breath with a wistful expression.

What was the point? She couldn't tell if this speech would end well for her.

"Dragons are rare," he began.

Yes, she was well aware of that. She wished he would get to the point.

"I have to admit, I'm intrigued by your idiosyncrasies."

What the hell did that mean? She quirked a brow.

"Let's have lunch to discuss how we can make your employment work best for your particular situation."

Rubbing the back of her neck, Alisa stared at him. "Uh," she stammered. "You want to like study me?"

He chuckled and let his head fall.

Her cheeks heated, and she swallowed hard. This was not what she had expected. Screaming, name-calling, maybe even throwing her out. Those seemed like appropriate responses, but asking to study her because she was uncommon? Definitely not.

"I'm sorry. I admit, that may have come out wrong." He held out his hands, palms up. "Allow me to rephrase. If you're interested in maintaining employment here, I would like that as well. But I'm not sure being a bartender will work."

Well, that was understandable.

"I'm starving and would like lunch, and since you're here, why don't we discuss it over food?" he asked.

"Oh." Her stomach rumbled as though to voice its agreement. "That makes more sense. Yeah. Let's do that. I could eat."

When *was* her last meal? She'd been so wrapped up in all the nonsense, she hadn't even stopped long enough to eat a banana. She was famished.

"There's this great little Mexican place. They have the best tapas." He pushed his chair back and stood.

"But how's their guacamole?" she countered, feeling at ease with him again.

Bringing his fingers to his lips, he made a kissing motion.

She chuckled.

"In the name of transparency, I'm trying to convince them to do a food truck so we can host them outside in the summer."

"So, this is a business lunch?" she asked as she stood.

Rounding his desk, he chuckled. "Of course!"

"Did you really just order one of everything off the tapas' menu?" Alisa chuckled at her boss.

He snorted. "I told you I was starving. Also, if I'm going to hire them to feed guests at my club, I need to sample what they have to offer. Besides, I come from a long line of good eaters. Is it different for you?"

"Well." She tucked some hair behind her ear with a shy grin. He had a point.

"Should we double it?" he asked.

The tension between them had dissipated while they walked to the restaurant. If she hadn't met his mate, she would think he was hitting on her, but she knew his kind mated for life. Some creatures out there were blessed with multiple mates, but crows weren't one of them.

As she lifted her margarita to her lips, she settled back into her chair. All the stress surrounding her job had evaporated. If she stayed in Manhattan, he'd employ her. Well, that was, if she survived her showdown with the Ember Witch.

Speaking of that...

Alisa glanced over her shoulder. Would that old wench do anything to her out in the open where humans could see? Or would she sneak up on her when she was alone again?

The most powerful coven in the world, and they were cowards. Her dragon snorted in agreement as she curled her tail around herself.

Then the wind shifted. It was nearly summer, late May, so there was absolutely no reason for there to be a hint of snow in the air. Her dragon perked within her and uncoiled her tail.

Oh shit. She knew that smell. Her dragon's excitement ramped up, but Alisa wasn't feeling the same. If anything, she stiffened.

This was not the right time.

As though it would do any good, she shifted her focus to the ground and ran her fingers along her forehead.

"Is everything okay?" Jason asked.

"What the fuck?" The thick baritone of his voice sent a shiver down her spine. She wasn't cold or even scared. Her dragon was intrigued. "This? Is this why you keep running away?"

125

27

DECLAN

S he couldn't be serious.

Declan's blood chilled. Ice pierced his throat, ready to explode from him. The dragon inside thrashed and bared his teeth. Another male had the audacity to be out on a date with *his* mate? His fingers curled into fists.

Jason. She chose Jason, the fragile *crow* shifter, over him? Sure, he had a kick-ass nightclub, but he could never compare to a *dragon*. He was a fucking bird!

His sow had her head down and her hand covering her face. "Oh my Gods, this cannot be happening," she muttered.

She didn't even have the nerve to look him in the eye.

"Alisa?" the club owner asked, leaning toward her cautiously with his gaze locked on Declan. "Is everything alright?"

Alisa? Was that her name? Jason knew, but her own *mate* didn't? What the actual fuck?

Declan's jaw tightened as his lips curled back into a snarl. "No. It's not."

Jason's brows furrowed.

The golden dragon, possibly named Alisa, turned toward him finally. "Do *not* make a scene," she whispered through clenched teeth, with ire burning in her eyes.

His cock twitched.

He'd make a scene, alright. If she didn't get the hell up from the table, he'd start flipping them, and that was just the start of what he'd do.

"Jason is my *boss*. I *work* at Fever. After last night." She took a deep breath, as though to calm her own emotions. "After last night, I needed to find out if I still had a job."

"And that requires a date?" Declan took a few steps closer, still glaring down at the crow.

"Excuse me?" Jason balked.

"This isn't." Alisa sprang to her feet to get between them.

"Two people having lunch together with drinks. That's a textbook date!" Declan's dragon screeched inside his skull, begged to be released so he could eviscerate the crow who dared get close to his mate.

When he attempted to tower over Jason, she shoved him back. "Enough! I told you it wasn't!"

Shifting his attention to his sow, he narrowed his eyes and inhaled deeply.

Did she carry his scent on her? If she did, so help him, Declan would lose his ever-loving mind. He definitely wouldn't be able to keep his beast tame.

"Then why do you keep running out after we rut?" he demanded.

Nothing. Just sunshine and ocean air. She smelled like herself with a hint of snow. A smile dared to creep on his lips. Declan's scent lingered on her.

Alisa's eyes widened, and she glanced around. "Do you have to be so godsdamned loud?"

"Are you ashamed?"

She covered her face. "I cannot deal with this right now."

"Alisa?" Jason said again as he stood, keeping distance between himself and Declan. "Do you need—"

"She doesn't need a thing from *you*." Declan jabbed his finger toward the crow.

Jason frowned and eyed him deadpan.

"Stop it!" Alisa screamed.

She turned toward the club owner, putting her back to Declan.

His muscles tightened. Rage chilled him as his scales threatened to break through his skin.

"I am so sorry. This is not how I expected any of this to go. Can we please touch base again about different positions within Fever tomorrow?"

"How about none?" Declan suggested.

"For the love of..." Alisa whirled toward him. "Shut your stupid mouth."

"How can you choose a crow over what fate gave you?" Declan commanded.

Was this the hex? Was that why she went on a date with the crow? The witch went on and on about how golden dragons cursed their mates. It was hard to follow, but either way, Jason could never compare to a dragon.

"I'm right here." Jason patted his chest and then extended his arms.

"And I'm wondering why that is exactly." Declan attempted to push Alisa aside so he could get at the club owner.

Unfortunately, or perhaps luckily, his mate wasn't exactly a delicate flower. She stood her ground and was an unmovable object. Was she protecting the crow?

"I already told you. Now, stop putting on this ridiculous display of macho-whatever. I'd like to keep my job, and you are ruining it for me." She took a deep breath and fixed her attention on Jason. "I'm really sorry. I need to deal with this."

This? Now he was just *this*?

Alisa wrapped her fingers around his wrist and yanked him in the opposite direction. "You want a fucking date. Fine! We will have a godsdamn date."

What did she just say? Confused and caught off-balance, Declan allowed his sow to tug him away from the club owner. Did she just declare they were going to go on a date?

Well, shit. That wasn't what he'd planned. Not that he'd had much time to come up with anything. He, honestly, was still working things out after leaving Felicity's place. Her aunt had definitely thrown a monkey wrench into his life.

He had so many questions for his mate, but he wouldn't say any of them were appropriate date conversation. Then again, what would be a better way to get them answered? If they were alone, instincts would take over. On a date, they could actually talk.

But where?

She had a decent hold on him and just dragged him through the city. Could he discuss what he wanted in mixed company? He'd have to try.

"Where are we going?" he asked.

28

ALISA

Alisa hadn't a clue where they were headed. She just knew the teal dragon couldn't be around Jason.

A date? He really thought after they had marked each other, she would just go out with another male? She snorted. That was a special kind of stupid logic.

"Well, you interrupted lunch, so I guess we're going to get food." That seemed like the most sensible destination.

He must've dug his heels in because their forward trajectory stopped. She bounced back and slammed into his chest. When he wrapped his arms around her, she assumed to catch her, her dragon swooned internally.

The stupid mongrel had been practically doing backflips since he showed up. She loved the dominant possessive asshole shit. Alisa could do without it.

"Heh." He nodded slightly. "Someone stopped me from enjoying a meal too. So, yeah. That sounds like a great idea."

Had a switch flipped or something? Where was his ire and rage? She swore he would've shifted right there on the street if she hadn't gotten him away from Jason. Now, he was all smooth and calm. It made no sense.

Despite herself, she inhaled deeply and reveled in a nose filled with his divine snowy scent. She lingered in his arms a moment, allowing her dragon to bask in their closeness. When he pressed his lips softly to her forehead, she remembered where they were—the middle of a sidewalk, under some scaffolding, in front of a laundromat. If they continued down that road, their dragon instincts would kick in. They wouldn't stop at small kisses.

Shaking her head as though to clear her mind, she pushed against him slightly, and his hold on her loosened. "Sorry."

His brows drew together.

She smoothed her hair nervously. "There's a pizzeria up the block." She gestured. "We can get a pie and hash this out in the park or something."

Without waiting for his answer, she turned and headed for the food. He followed. They were mates, and if his dragon was anything like hers, he'd despise the distance between them.

"You can't do shit like that," she scolded when she felt his presence behind her.

"What?"

"You can't be all macho asshole in front of my boss. I need to work. Besides, he's mated." Couldn't he tell? Every female in a twenty-mile radius could.

The teal dragon behind her grumbled. "How am I supposed to know that?"

"You can't smell it?"

"Not really."

She peered over her shoulder at him.

He shrugged. "I'm straight. I don't look at dudes that way. So why would I care if he was mated or not? I do not need to scent his mating."

She opened her mouth to rebut him, but she had nothing. After bringing her lips together and looking away, she had to admit he had a point. If he couldn't sense it, she could admit it looked a bit date-like.

"And if you don't want me to be possessive, maybe you shouldn't keep running away from me, being hot and cold. It's confusing."

Chewing her bottom lip, she lowered her gaze. "This whole thing is baffling."

His hand found hers. Glancing toward their joined palms briefly, she stopped and turned toward him.

"Then let's hash it out," he suggested in the sincerest tone, wearing the most innocent expression.

Her heart melted.

They had to talk. There'd be no way they could be mates without a discussion. She just didn't know what to say. So, instead of using her words, she nodded.

His smile warmed her chest. Squeezing his hand, they continued on their way hand in hand, side by side.

In silence, they walked the few blocks to the pizzeria. Clouds might have rolled in, and the barometric pressure dipped slightly, but Alisa found comfort in being beside the teal dragon. They didn't need to fill the quiet with words. When her shoulder brushed his arm, the tiniest of shivers rippled through her. It put a smile on her face.

His company felt natural. For the first time since her arrival in Manhattan, she was calm. It was nice. If this was mating, she could get used to it.

When they arrived at the small restaurant, he trotted ahead. Pulling the door open, he bowed and gestured. "After you."

A small giggle escaped from her. She had no experience with dating. It didn't seem to be that imperative, especially when she was a slave to her heat. So, minute chivalrous gestures like his were quite the novelty to her.

Dipping her chin, she made her way inside. "Thank you."

There was nothing like the smell of garlic, tomatoes, and mozzarella. The scent of delicious Italian food wrapped itself around Alisa, and her stomach rumbled loudly. She was famished.

"What do you like on your pizza?" Declan asked as he approached the counter.

"D!" the petite young human woman behind the counter exclaimed upon seeing him. "So good to see you. You getting the usual?"

Her eyes sparkled, and she wore a grin from ear to ear. She was definitely fond of him. Alisa's scales vibrated beneath her skin. Flames flared in her chest. Her dragon snarled in her mind.

Alisa's mate licked his bottom lip as he dropped his head slightly. His gaze drifted toward her briefly before returning to the counter lady. "Nah. I was thinking maybe two pies and some wings."

He reached for Alisa and tenderly draped his arm over her shoulders in a subtle, possessive gesture.

Alisa glared at the pizzeria worker, unable to control her dragon's jealous nature.

"Oh." The pink tinge in the clerk's cheeks had nothing to do with the temperature in the shop.

"So..." Declan focused on Alisa. "What would you like? Are you a pepperoni kind of woman or veggie lover?" He wrinkled his face playfully.

Leaning into him, accepting his affection, she considered her options. Pursing her lips, she glanced at the menu as though this pizzeria would offer anything different from any other. "I definitely could use some protein. So, like, a sausage…" her voice trailed off.

"A meat lovers?" he offered with a sly grin.

Chuckling, she covered her face. She'd walked right into that one. "Yeah," she agreed with a sigh.

He nodded. "Two meaty delights and a dozen hot and honey wings."

The woman behind the counter tapped the register and jotted it down on the pad. She gave a price, and when Alisa reached for her wallet, Declan stood between Alisa and the counter to pay. No words passed between them, but she understood and let him pay.

They went to a small booth as the place filled with people eager to get their lunch orders. "So." She took a deep inhale. "What do you do?"

That seemed like an appropriate place to start their date conversation.

Thunder boomed outside, and she glanced over her shoulder. Great. A storm rolled in.

"Brand and content marketing for Arach Jewelry."

Alisa snapped back toward him with wide eyes. He did *not* just say that.

"You okay?" he asked.

Blinking, she tucked some hair behind her ear and looked away. She needed to play this off. "They're just the best jewelry *ever*. How did you land a job like that?" Working for her father. Seriously, what were the odds?

He lifted a shoulder. "Friends of the family." He sounded so nonchalant about it. "I mean, there aren't many of us around," he whispered. "So, we kind of help each other out, you feel me?"

She swallowed hard. Of course, she knew their kind was scarce. "Ah." She nodded. What else could she say?

"And you?" Before she could answer, he slapped his face. "Duh. You said you work at Fever."

She pushed away the awkwardness and grinned at him. "Yes. I was a bartender, but that might not be the case anymore. So, Jason wanted to help me find a different position within his company."

He hummed and tapped the table. His gaze flicked from her to behind her, then back again. "I don't think the talk we need to have can be had here." He swirled his finger in the air, indicating several humans around them. "And while a picnic in the park would've been a great idea, I don't think either of us want soggy pizza and wings."

He had yet another good point. He really needed to stop doing that. "Okay, so what do you suggest?"

He brought his hands together and rubbed them as he glanced toward the counter.

Was he looking at the human again? Alisa's blood heated once more. Her dragon snorted in her mind. She'd rip that woman limb from limb if she had to.

"My place isn't too far," he offered with his attention back to her. "You up for that?"

29

DECLAN

Color Declan surprised, but Alisa agreed to go to his apartment with him. Now, to be fair, she had to know her safety wasn't in question. They were mates. There would be no possible way he could harm her. His dragon simply wouldn't allow it.

They needed privacy to discuss their mating. Humans couldn't hear about it. Their existence was hidden from them. Neither one of them wanted to face the consequences of that. So, yes, his place—since it was closer—was the most logical option. As long as they kept their dragons in check, they could actually have a conversation.

The two of them sat cross-legged on the floor of his living room with the large square coffee table between them. A pile of wing bones sat in the white carton on top of an empty pizza box with a half-eaten pie remaining in another container.

They'd covered the basics while waiting for the food and on their walk to his place—where they grew up, what they did for fun, and various favorites. With that out of the way, he was more comfortable delving into the deeper details.

Mostly, he wanted to learn more about this curse, but how did he approach that? It seemed rude to just say it without some sort of segue.

"I know a lot of dragons prefer the space found in mountains," Declan began as he tried to figure out a good way to approach the topic. "My family lives in the Rockies of Colorado, and you said you're from Upstate New York. What brought you to Manhattan?"

She leaned back, pulled up her knees, and wrapped her arms around them. He suspected she was contemplating her answer. Which seemed odd. It wasn't a hard question.

"My mom died when I was very young. My grandmother raised me. So I've had kind of a lonely existence." She frowned, and his heart pinched. "I found out my dad is here, and I wanted to meet him."

"No shit." He nodded. "Is he a dragon too?" Declan suspected she was full-blooded, but with the rarity of their kind, it wasn't guaranteed.

"Yeah." She kept her gaze on the pizza slices when she spoke. "Are both your parents dragons also?"

"My mom is a water dragon, and my dad is ice," he offered. "My half sister Scarlett is older than me, and she's a fire dragon. She mated with a bear. Tessa, my younger sister, is ice like me."

Her expression brightened, and she met his gaze. "Sisters? That's cool."

"So, your dad is here. I take it your parents weren't mates?" he prodded.

Her smile faded, and she shifted. It seemed like she wanted to make herself smaller or something. His inner beast went on guard, and a need to comfort her overwhelmed him.

Had he just stumbled on the curse? Was this his opening to start that conversation?

Scooting around the table, he positioned himself to her left. Curling two fingers under her chin, he coaxed her to lift her eyes to meet his. "I won't think less of you. I mean, it happens. We're dragons. Scarlett has a different father than me. I get it."

She tightened her lips together. The pain reflected in her features sent a knife through his heart. The animal inside him seethed. He wanted to tear the throat out of whomever put that expression on her face.

She swallowed hard. "No," she said on a sigh. "I don't know much, but what I have learned is that it was extremely complicated."

The way she said *complicated* gave the impression it was an understatement. Declan shimmied closer and wrapped an arm around her. When he pulled her in for a hug, she nuzzled against him. His heart swelled, and his dragon, though still on guard, settled slightly and flicked his tail.

With her head tucked under his chin, he shut his eyes and reveled in their closeness while running his fingers through her hair.

"From what I'm told, they wanted to be mates and tried to choose mating."

Declan inhaled deeply, getting a lungful of her salty sea air scent.

"But my father had a fated mate, and she found him."

"That's rough. My parents are chosen mates, not fated. They work really hard on their relationship. They've said it's a lot of effort to get fate to accept their choice. I can't imagine what it would be like to start that process only to have it derailed."

She blew out a pained breath. "My mother didn't take it well, and it's kind of how she died."

When she pushed him, he furrowed his brow. Loosening his grip, he allowed her to pull away despite his dragon grumbling in his mind.

She peered up at him with a sullen expression. "What do you know about golden dragons?"

Declan cocked his head to the side. This was his opportunity to ask about the curse.

"Honestly, not much other than you're rare—like the rarest of rare creatures." He licked his bottom lip, bracing himself to broach the topic. Now or never. "But I heard a rumor recently."

Her lips tightened into a thin line, and worry creased her features. While she said nothing, he could feel her anxiety. He had to continue and explain.

He had to preface this with an explanation to give her context. "So, my best friend, he got mated not that long ago to a human." Maybe he went too far back. Clearing his throat, he tried again. "Okay, so she has a friend, and she's a witch. Apparently, her aunt is an Ember Witch."

When her face went white and her eyes widened, his heart stopped.

"Okay, by the look on your face, I assume what she said is true. You're cursed?"

She shoved at him. The surprise was gone. Fire burned in her irises as she scrambled to her feet. "You told the witch I was here!"

"What?" He fell back, startled by her change in mood.

"That old bitch witch tried to run me out of Manhattan! You're the reason."

"Me?" He placed a hand on his chest. "I didn't tell her anything about you."

Alisa narrowed her eyes at him and planted her hands on her hips. "Then how the fuck did she find out?"

He climbed to his feet. "I haven't a clue. She's a witch. They're magical and communicate with the fates."

"You're my mate!" she shouted. "You're supposed to protect me!"

Her words stabbed him through the chest, and he gaped at her. "How did I not?"

Shaking her head, she crossed her arms over her chest. Moving away from him, she paced his living room, chewing on the inside of her cheek.

At least she didn't run away. He'd count that as a win. Time to regroup. The only way he could understand all of it was to start from the beginning. "What is the curse?"

She pursed her lips together.

"I'm your mate. If you're cursed, I am too. I should know what we're fighting."

"What?"

"We're mates. Any challenges are our challenges—not yours or mine. They're both of ours. That's how this works."

She blinked several times and opened her mouth, but only stuttered noises came out.

Declan closed the distance between them and placed his hands reassuringly on her shoulders. He stooped slightly so he could look directly into her eyes. She needed to understand his commitment to their mating.

"Whatever it is, we face it together. If it's witches, so be it. Fate is on our side." Not to mention, he was pretty sure he could rally his friends to help. Gideon and Ella definitely hadn't forgiven Felicity's aunt for tossing her off a cliff. It wouldn't take much to get them on their side. "Tell me everything about this curse."

30

ALISA

The resolve in Declan's voice made it easy to let the details of Alisa's curse spill from her. She held nothing back. The burden she bore felt lighter when she shared it with him, and she stood taller in the face of it.

Her dragon trusted Declan. It was her human half that was slow to get on board. As a shifter, she needed to accept her instincts were better than her gut. Mating was the one area her dragon knew better than her human. Besides, Declan wasn't all that bad.

He didn't offer judgment as she shared about how she'd endured her heat mercilessly because the witches denied her the protection elixir. While she didn't get into the dirty details about her mother, she informed him that her entire line was cursed and, by extension, any mates they chose, including him.

He didn't interject. Instead, he leaned in, studied her, and offered her hugs with back rubs. Despite sharing her curse with him, he showed her nothing but affection. This warmed not just her dragon's heart toward him, but her human one as well. This could possibly work, if she got her human head out of her ass.

Maybe fate had forgiven golden dragons. Biting her lip, she was reluctant to let that spark of hope burn too bright. They still had to come up with a plan for what to do about the Ember Witches.

Feeling safe with him, she went on. She explained how the witch showed up at her apartment and threatened her.

"She's an unethical witch," he muttered.

He'd been so silent until then. She hadn't expected him to have a comment on the witch, but his words reaffirmed what her dragon already knew—Declan was trustworthy.

"I've met her the once, and I've heard she used fate as an excuse to do things no one in their right mind would."

His words begged the question, and it slipped past her lips before she could stop the words. "What did she do?"

Could it be as bad as what her mother had done or what had caused the curse for all golden dragons? Alisa doubted it, but maybe he had something that could help them fight. The Ember Witches had this reputation of being above reproach. Maybe this one witch was acting on her own.

Alisa's mind spun with possibilities, but she needed to focus on her mate. He had valuable information.

Taking a deep breath, he guided her to the couch. "She shoved my friend's mate off a cliff right in front of him."

Alisa's eyes widened. "What? Why?" That should've been a death sentence for the Ember Bitch.

Holding her hands in his lap, he shook his head. "Some lame excuse about it being the only way to get them to accept their mating. Believe me, they haven't forgiven her."

"How could they?" Alisa blurted. She'd just recently heard about it, and she was pissed on their behalf.

"I agree." He squeezed her hand, and she felt it around her heart.

"Wait." She slid a hand out of his and held it up. "What makes you think it's the same witch?"

She suspected it was, but there was a small possibility it wasn't. The Ember Witch Coven was quite large. She needed to know for sure just how many were against her. Was it one rogue magic bearer or the entire coven?

He cleared his throat and reclaimed her hand. "She's my other friend's aunt. I don't know how we work around that, but we will find a way."

Her dragon snapped her jaws within her. Alisa was convinced she wasn't trustworthy. Of course, she was related to the woman who wanted Alisa and everyone close to her dead.

She needed to calm the rage brewing inside her. She had to hear him out. This wasn't the time to jump to conclusions. She should start with clarifying questions.

"The woman I saw you with at Fever?" She'd had a magical aura around her. That had to be the friend of which he spoke.

He nodded. "Yeah. We're just friends."

She pursed her lips. Her inner beast snarled.

His eyes widened. "We've never even slept together. I admit, we hooked up a little, but we never actually rutted." The words came so quickly she barely caught them all.

It shouldn't have mattered. They were shifters, and sex was a natural thing. She wasn't exactly a virgin herself. But then again, jealousy ran deep with mates. So, she felt better knowing he hadn't been intimate with the witch.

"Witches are loyal to one another—above all else. Why do you think they have covens? They stick together." Something about this didn't sit right with her. She shook her head. "I get she's your friend, but you even said the Ember Witch is her blood."

Alisa stood, wringing her hands. The more she thought about it, the more anxious she became. Pacing in his apartment, she bit her bottom lip.

"It's not like that." He jumped up and followed her. "I swear. Trust me, she isn't fond of her aunt's ways."

Her inner dragon grumbled and shook her head. The beast inside her didn't like the idea of the witch, either. It didn't smell right. He just happened to be friends with a relative of the witch who sought to end Alisa?

Okay, well, to be fair, it did make some sense. If the magical ones spent any time together as family, they would be in Manhattan. So, yeah, Alisa being in Manhattan, it meant there was an increased likelihood they would cross paths.

Fine.

It wasn't entirely out of the question.

Declan placed his hands on her arms and rubbed them gently up and down. "You told me fate punished golden dragons and rid the world of their mates. Felicity's aunt echoed that, but if destiny brought us together, and we are mates by destiny, then your line has been forgiven. The Ember Witches call themselves the guardians of fate. They preach you cannot interfere with it. Wouldn't their objection to your existence and our union be the exact opposite of their purpose?"

She bit her lip and studied his intense expression. Her brows drew together. She wanted to believe his words. Everything he said sounded logical. "The witches are bitter."

"Let them be," he said and swooshed his hand away dismissively. "We have destiny on our side. They cannot combat that."

She wanted it to be as easy as he explained, but deep in her bones, she knew it wouldn't be. There'd be a battle. Loyalties would be on the line. Would his friend pick him or her coven?

Would he choose his mate over the rest of the world? There was her human half doubting him again. Her dragon believed in him and their bond, so why couldn't her human brain get with the program?

Alisa had to be a realist. She didn't have the luxury of living in a fantasy filled with denial. She'd existed every day of her life under the thumb of the Ember Witches. The world was against her.

But not Declan. If she truly looked at his actions, she'd see he has been on her side the whole time.

Could this be fate's cruel twist? It gave her a mate only to have her suffer further when the Ember Witches stole him from her. There'd be no way she could survive that. It had killed her mother, and it wasn't fair to do to Declan.

"You have to understand, by mating me, you have brought the ire of the Ember Witches upon you too. It's why golden dragons don't have partners for long. Fate abolished our true mates."

"Until now," he interjected.

Sorrow filled her. Hope radiated from him. It was clear he didn't understand. So she continued. "But we could still find another."

"Our mating is solid," he insisted. "Ours is fate!"

She swallowed and nodded. "But that wasn't always the case. For many generations, it's been the opposite. It wasn't enough for us to be denied the natural order. The Ember Witches stole our mates and murdered them once we chose one. I didn't know it at the time, but I do now. You have to understand, they aren't just after me, they're going to get you too."

She hated the way the words tasted on her tongue, but they had to be said. Nothing hurt more than understanding the consequences laid out before her. Yes, they were destined for each other, but that didn't come without costs.

"Being tied to me is a death sentence, and I'm sorry I couldn't protect you from it."

Her heart pinched, and her throat went dry. She'd finally found the relief to her anguish. Her heat could no longer torment her, but in doing so, she'd put him directly in the line of fire.

How much more fucked up could her life be? The price wasn't worth it.

To her surprise and confusion, his eyes sparkled as he grinned down at her. He should be shaking in his boots. Mating her was a death sentence. What was he so happy about?

His hand slid to her hips, and he pulled her against his chest. Immediately, her inner beast perked, and her core tingled. Being this close to him sparked her arousal despite the temperature of the conversation.

"Let them come for me." Declan dropped to one knee. "We are mates. Our bond is new but strong. Nothing can break what fate has brought together. Let the witches try. I am yours. You are mine. Death to anyone who tries to steal that from us."

31

DECLAN

As Declan knelt before Alisa, his head at the height of her belly, his dragon stirred. It wasn't as simple as being near his mate and the beast being interested in rutting. No. He sensed something. The animal within him narrowed his eyes and pressed against the barrier, holding him inside his human form.

What was he trying to hear?

Following his lead, Declan did the same. He leaned against Alisa's stomach, his ear to her softness. The slight hint of her arousal tickled his nose. His dick thickened slightly but nothing he couldn't handle. More important things needed their focus. As he held her close, he caught a sound.

A faint... what was that?

His fingers dug into her as he inched that much closer. There wasn't much space between them—whatever existed, he ate it up. They were fully pressed against each other.

Would he hear it again?

"Declan?" she asked. "This feels weird. I mean, at first it was romantic and all. But now."

"Shh." He brought a finger to his lips.

There!

Holy shit.

Pulling away slightly, he gaped at her stomach.

"What?" Panic crept into her tone.

This just got real. He marveled at her, and reality punched him in the gut. It made him smile. On a primal level, this was the whole point. However, on a human level—as people with stuff going on and plans—this was essentially unexpected. Not that he took any measures to prevent it.

"Declan!" she shouted, breaking into his thoughts. "What's with the goofy look on your face? Why are you staring at me like that?"

He cocked his head to the side as he rose to his full height. With elation coursing through his veins, he wrapped his arms around her, and he kissed the top of her head. "You can't feel it?"

Never, in all his life, had an adult milestone made him experience this much joy. It had happened. Everything would change that much more, and he couldn't contain his glee.

"You'll have to be more specific. It's been a crazy few days. I've been sensing a lot of things."

How could she not tell? Moving to stand beside her, he splayed his fingers and laid them on her stomach as he met her gaze. He'd be doing that a lot over the coming weeks.

Eyes wide as saucers, she gaped. Stammering incoherently, she placed her hand over his. "No," she finally muttered. "It's impossible. I—" She paused mid-sentence and canted her head slightly as though considering.

While she sorted it out in her mind, he slipped his hand from beneath hers and let her touch her own belly. He couldn't stop smiling. His dragon puffed his chest and preened with pride.

Declan rolled his eyes internally. Yes. The beast had done what his instincts told him to do, and both he and his inner animal were ecstatic about it.

It wasn't planned, but he'd make it work. Fate dealt them this card, and they sure as shit were going to play it to the best of their ability. Their bonding might feel like breakneck speed, but that was mating for his kind. The whole point of the mating grounds and hearing the calls was to make new dragons.

They'd done it.

Alisa was with egg. She'd have his child. Declan would be a father.

It was trippy as hell.

"But I—" She shook her head. "Fuck."

Wait. She wasn't happy. Swallowing down his glee, which was definitely a hard pill to get down, he hugged her tight. He might not have understood her lack of excitement, he knew enough to attempt to comfort her.

"I didn't get more Plan B. I didn't do my thing the second time. Stuff has been so out of control I just never picked any up. You can't just buy it in bulk."

Stroking her hair, he once again kissed the crown of her head. "We'll figure it out."

She pushed at his chest. "How?"

Definitely not the response he anticipated. This was what mating was all about. Especially for dragons. In the face of her accusatory stare, he scrambled to come up with how they would make having an egg together work.

"Off the top of my head? We'll share custody."

Okay, that probably wasn't the best response, but what did she expect? The way she peered at him definitely gave him the impression she wasn't appreciating his humanlike response to their shifter problem.

This was a first time for him. Shit. He really was maturing.

Shaking her head, she stepped away from him and ran her fingers through her own hair.

That definitely didn't bode well for him. He braced himself for what she'd say.

"A witch is trying to kill us, end golden dragons, and we're going to have an egg? This isn't a custody dispute, Declan. This is about safety and surviving!"

Frowning, she had him there. Declan's beast reared inside him at the mere mention of something wanting to harm his mate and their soon-to-be egg. But he refused to believe fate would give him a mate *and* an egg only to take it from them. No. That wasn't how any of this worked. One of them had to be positive, and it would be him.

"We have time before the egg actually gets here."

She glared at him. "Six weeks!" Her hand remained on her stomach. "That isn't enough. We'll never get away from an Ember Witch." She chewed on her bottom lip. "I mean, it's protected inside me, but after that…" Her voice trailed off, and the color drained from her face.

Were those tears? That just wouldn't do.

His dragon was on high alert. He snarled at whatever had caused his mate to potentially cry.

Declan, the human portion anyway, reached for her and hugged her to his chest. "I will protect you *and* our egg."

If he kept saying it, he'd manifest safety for his soon-to-be family.

"How could this happen?" she asked, burying her face in his chest.

Taking ahold of her face with both hands, he pulled back. "We did this because it is our instinct, our nature to mate and then make more dragons. We can keep this egg and eventual hatchling safe. Have faith in us and fate. Destiny wouldn't have allowed it if we couldn't handle it."

Searching her eyes, fear reflected back at him. Not one ounce of excitement or even hope. She was absolutely terrified. His dragon raged inside him. He wanted to destroy whomever instilled this emotion in her and robbed her of the joy at finding out she carried an egg.

He needed to ease it. His words had fallen on deaf ears. There had to be another strategy.

Dipping his head down, he paused, hovering his lips over hers. "I vow, with every fiber of my being, with every breath in my lungs, that we will have a successful mating and a healthy dragon child. You and our hatchling will be safe."

Closing his eyes, he went the final way and kissed her with every bit of tenderness he had within him.

32

ALISA

With his hands on either side of Alisa's face, he forced her to focus on him. All the panic, disbelief, and shock she felt in the face of finding out she carried an egg melted away. Studying his brown eyes and how they shifted to a soft blue signaled that not only did his human look upon her with the utmost affection but so did his dragon. Her heart pinched, her stomach flipped, and her sex heated. Her own beast swooned in delight.

This was the purpose of the mating call. She'd done the impossible. Her golden line would continue. With her mate by her side, she could conquer the witches.

His vow brushed lightly over her lips before he sealed his promise with a kiss. Never in all her life had she felt so utterly and completely cherished. Practically a puddle, she leaned into him. She snaked her arms around his middle, holding on to him—and their moment. They had a tough battle ahead of them. The Ember Witches definitely wouldn't go down easily. This might be their last moment of peace and happiness before they went to war.

His hands dropped from her face, trailed along her neck, over her shoulders, and to her hips. His fingertips cooled the growing inferno beneath her skin and made her shudder. Their kiss broke, and he pulled away, offering her a sweet, sensual smile.

As though he heard her thoughts—could he? Did mates have that ability? No. That couldn't be. Could it? Internally, she shook off the distraction as he dug his fingers into her and lifted her.

Instinctively, she wrapped her legs around him and hooked her ankles behind his back. She circled his shoulders with her arms and held him tight, unable to contain her gleeful grin as he carried her out of the living room. It seemed he wanted to revel in their moment just as much as she did.

Burying her face into his neck, she showered him with soft pecks, ensuring she paid special attention to the slightly raised scar from the mating mark she'd given him. That bite had solidified their destined bond. The fates had forgiven golden dragons. There was no other explanation.

All they had to do was to defeat the Ember Witches. They were the only threat to their eternal bliss.

Her stomach flipped, and a squeal escaped her when he tossed her. The half a second she flew before landing on a cloud of bedding knocked the danger they faced from her mind.

Lying on her back, in the middle of a king-sized bed with the softest duvet she'd ever experience, she giggled. Arousal, nerves, and anticipation for what was to come bubbled inside her.

Standing at the foot of the bed, he ran his hand along his chin and licked his bottom lip. His gaze drank her in, and she felt like the tastiest morsel on a dessert display.

"You know the cliché of a pregnant woman glowing?" he asked in a thick, feral voice.

She tilted her head as she lifted herself up on her elbows. "Where are you going with this?"

"I really thought it was just something people said."

With a furrowed brow, she blinked up at him. "Okay?"

Half a chuckle came from deep within his chest before he bent, hovering over her. "You have an aura. It's subtle but magnificent."

Again, his lips gently met her own for too brief a second of tenderness before drifting up to her forehead. When he graced her with another loving kiss, any reservations she had about him evaporated.

This was her mate. Fate blessed their union with an egg. There wasn't a logical reason to resist it.

"Now," he said, kissing the tip of her nose.

She snickered.

"Without further ado, may I worship you?"

Her throat went dry, and her core burned with a fiery need for him. If he said another thing, she might just dissolve into a pool of lava right there on his bed.

Then again, that might be his intention.

She ran her tongue along her bottom lip and inhaled deeply, savoring the scent of him and their mingled arousal. He craved her just as much as she did him. "As you wish."

He waggled his brows before scooting down the bed. With the most meticulous care—and patience she had never witnessed before—he removed every single article of clothing she wore individually. As each inch of skin was revealed, he paused and showered her body with adoration.

He alternated between his lips, soft licks, and gentle grazes of his teeth. Each sensual touch sent tingles bolting through her and straight to her sex. She squirmed and moaned. With her eyes closed, she basked in his attention.

No one in her life had ever devoted so much time and care to her body. The mating grounds weren't meant for anything resembling this. Each coupling had been quick, mostly violent trysts, that left her sated but never feeling cherished.

Declan's focus on her—his attention to every nook and cranny of her figure—meant she discovered new areas that caused her toes to curl. Once he rolled her to her stomach, biting and massaging the globes of her ass, she'd nearly lost her mind.

It tickled but also made her pussy quake with need. She clawed at his sheets and arched her back when his tongue trailed her spine.

She gasped the moment his thick cockhead pressed against her slick opening. Lost in the sensations, she hadn't really paid attention to where he'd positioned his body, just where he touched her. His chest pressed against her back, cooling her molten skin as he slid the length of his stiff cock deep inside her.

Rolling her hips, she did her best to meet him. She groaned, feeling every inch of him stretching her walls to accommodate his girth. She burned white-hot beneath his cool body. The contrast of their elements made her head spin.

Resting on his elbows, he slowly buried himself inside her. Fully seated, he pressed his lips to her ear. His chilly breath, combined with the fullness of him inside her, caused her to shudder.

"Made for me," he whispered.

She quivered under him.

"A perfect fit."

Gods. She could die right now and be dreamily at peace.

Painfully slow, he withdrew himself from her, and she whined. With just the tip of his cock lingering at her opening, she wiggled her ass to entice him. She needed him inside her again. Her dragon, her soul, begged for him to drive himself deep again.

"Easy, my golden goddess," he rumbled in her ear. "I want to savor you. We don't need to rush. We have all night and then some to enjoy each other."

As delightful as that sounded, Alisa craved the rough manner he'd rutted her before.

Whimpering, she tried to urge him again. "More."

Chuckling, he dropped his head, and his chest bounced slightly against her back. Without saying a word, he plunged himself hard and fast inside her.

The movement stole her breath. She saw stars. Placing his palms on her shoulder blades, pinning her down on his bed, he pounded her hard and fast.

"Just the way my mate wants it," he ground out between clenched teeth.

With each inward thrust, he drove her deep into the mattress and shoved her closer to the edge. She squeezed her eyes shut, unable to focus on anything other than the feeling of his swollen, thick cock drilling her.

Held in place by his weight, she couldn't do more than scream and receive the relentless fucking. There was a moment where she lost connection with reality and drifted off to a place of pure bliss.

They'd rutted before, but never had she felt so close to the surface of the sun. Every muscle in her body tightened. Pain mingled with pleasure as she teetered on the edge.

Right there. Just like that.

The earth shattered, and she bellowed his name. Shouting at the top of her lungs, every ounce of tension she'd experienced her entire life released the moment her orgasm barreled into her and rocketed her to another plane of existence.

Her grandmother had explained the mate bond. She'd understood it on a surface level. No one could have prepared her for cementing her union with Declan.

33

DECLAN

There was no sleep deeper, nor restful, than a night spent beside Declan's mate. He never had to add an extra blanket. The chills never came. The golden fire dragon beside him warmed him to the core.

Alisa. Her name was just as beautiful as she was. In both forms, human and dragon, she was magnificent. Alisa. He loved the sound of it.

Spooning, he lay on his side. One arm was beneath her neck. Her pert little ass was tucked against his morning erection. Draped over her hip, his hand rested on her soft belly.

The idea of it swelling over the next few weeks with his egg filled him with such elation he could explode. He'd never even fathomed this level of happiness. Of course, he had heard about the sheer joy that was mating, but this? This was off the charts.

It was almost enough for him to forget the curse business.

Dammit.

As the morning light poured in his bedroom window, reality came with it. They didn't get a simple happy ever after. They had a battle with a nasty old bitch of an Ember Witch. One that didn't fight fair.

They'd already defied the curse—they were fated mates. Declan might be new to dealing with the Ember Witches, but he was familiar enough about them to understand they didn't take kindly to being defied.

Reinforcements were necessary. It'd be the only way they could win over an Ember Witch. The more the better. He and his mate didn't have to do this alone. He had friends.

Keeping his one arm under his woman, he rolled onto his back and reached for his phone on the nightstand.

When she shifted, obviously realizing he'd moved, he paused. He didn't mean to wake her. They'd rutted through most of the night. She should be dead to the world, but he didn't want to take any chances. Besides, she'd earned her rest. She would grow his egg. And with what they were to face in the coming days, she'd need every ounce of energy to fight.

Once she let out a lazy groan and shimmied her ass against his hip, he grinned. She was still sleeping deeply.

With his free hand, he grabbed his phone. Using his thumb, he unlocked it and swiped through to find the group text he had with his friends. Normally, he despised it, but it came in handy recently.

Tap. Tap. Tap. He fired off a quick message that he needed help on an urgent matter. As vague as it was, he didn't want to put his and Alisa's dilemma all out there like that. Explaining everything in person, so they truly understood, was the only way. He trusted them. They'd understand, show up. In the next hour, his kitchen would be full of support. Now, the question was, what was he to do with the next sixty minutes?

Rolling back into place, he hugged his mate against him. It wouldn't be long before his apartment would be filled with questions and panic. He should savor the peace and quiet while it lasted. Besides, Alisa deserved more sleep. She'd been through hell, but nothing seemed to relax her more than rutting. He *was* at full attention. His dragon champed at the bit for another opportunity to sample his mate, but was it the best idea?

Closing his eyes, he moved his hips, allowing his thick erection to slip in the crease between her cheeks. So soft and plush. His woman was a gift from the gods for sure—his. He didn't know what he'd done so right in his life to deserve such a magnificent woman, but he'd spend the rest of his days devoted to worshipping his golden goddess.

As she stirred, she pushed her ass back against him. Maybe a reflex? Instincts? It didn't matter, he'd accept that as consent. His hands found her hips before she could turn into him.

"Don't," he whispered into her ear.

Shimmying in the bed, he positioned himself. It didn't take long before the tip of his cock found her hot well of arousal. Without a second thought, he thrust his hips forward and filled her. She gasped and quivered against him.

The best feeling in the world. Her walls clenched around him as though trying to pull him deeper.

Rutting his female every chance he got was his new favorite activity.

Alisa

Sore and sated—the perfect way to start a morning. If this was mating, then Alisa was all in. Her teal dragon was far more talented than she had ever imagined a male could be. Not only that, but after he'd brought her to another plane of existence, he was in the kitchen making *breakfast* while she showered.

The smells of French toast, bacon, and eggs wafted toward the bathroom, making her mouth water. Good thing too. The sex had left her absolutely famished. Plus, she ate for two now. The idea he'd made her a buffet of some of the best foods in the world made her heart swell.

This was the life the Ember Witches wanted to deny her. Her inner beast whipped her tail inside Alisa's mind. She was ready to fight for not only her mate but their egg—a future for every golden dragon. As the soapy suds ran down her body, she covered her stomach. What was inside challenged the Ember Witches and needed to be protected no matter what.

Closing her eyes, she inhaled deeply. The water cascaded down around her in the shower as she braced herself for battle. She had six weeks to end this. It had to be enough. It was all they had. There'd be no way she could fight a witch and protect an egg simultaneously. Eggs were far too fragile.

As she turned in the stall and lifted her face to meet the spray, muffled voices caught her ear. Snapping her head toward the bathroom door, she leaned in. Her dragon stood at attention. She narrowed her eyes as though that would make listening easier.

With preternatural hearing, she should've been able to make out what was said or identify the voices. With the water rushing and echoing off the shower walls, she could only pick up people speaking—not what they were saying.

Who would Declan have over this early? Then again, it was afternoon, so it wasn't completely absurd. But seriously. Who would show up at his place unannounced? No sane person would invite over a group of people after spending his night screwing his mate.

She froze under the spray.

The Ember Witch.

She could have shown up.

With her hackles raised and her relaxing shower ruined, Alisa cautiously turned off the water and exited the shower. After she twisted a towel atop her head, she wrapped another one around her body.

As this little sleepover hadn't been planned, she could only put on the clothes from the previous day. That was fine. She actually hadn't been wearing them that long. Wait! Where were they? Shit. She glanced toward his dresser. He was larger than her. Maybe she could throw on some of his clothes. They were mates. It shouldn't be a big deal.

Her dragon snapped her jaws upon hearing a female's voice. What in the ever-loving hell? A woman? He invited a woman over? Rage boiled in her veins as she ripped open the top drawer and snatched some boxers from inside. The drawer below it had T-shirts. Perfect. As she dressed quickly, she noted the conversation in the other room had gone from boisterous and jovial to soft and whispered. It was so low her supernatural hearing couldn't make out words.

Secrets? What the hell was going on? Obviously, he was aware she'd be able to listen to them. By speaking in such hushed tones, she assumed it was purposeful. They didn't want Alisa to know of what they spoke. What were they hiding? Who were they?

Not being able to hear them fed the jealous fury burning inside her chest. The scales beneath her skin scraped over each other as she moved. Her dragon roared in her brain. Something wasn't right about this.

Ripping the door to his bedroom open with her teeth clenched, Alisa practically stomped into the living area of Declan's apartment. With her fists clenched, her shoulders bunched, and her teeth grinding, she surveyed the room.

Declan's witch friend, Alisa's half brother, and his mate stood in the kitchen area. His friends. Declan had his back to her but twisted quickly to see her.

His friend's magic radiated off her and reached out to Alisa. Reflexively, she attempted to swipe it away.

He'd invited a witch into his apartment while she was in the shower. Alisa vibrated with ire. Her dragon wailed for release.

A tiny voice in her head begged her to hear him out. Her mate wouldn't put her in danger on purpose. But his trust in his witch friend hadn't sat well with her last night, and it only felt worse now that she stood face-to-face with her.

Declan rushed to her and placed his hands on her shoulders. His gaze darted around her features. Worry creased his brow.

"Alisa?" He crouched to fully make eye contact with her and thoroughly blocked her view of his friends. "They're here to help."

Her eye twitched as again the aura surrounding the female witch tried to entangle itself around Alisa. "She's casting."

"What?" Her mate straightened his spine. "Felicity, stop!" he shouted over his shoulder.

"I'm not doing anything." The witch held her hands up, palms toward them, but the glow about them shone brighter.

The dragon deep within Alisa's chest rumbled, and a growl escaped her curled lips. "Liar."

"What's going on?" asked the only human in the room.

Alisa's half brother stepped in front of her, putting himself between the woman and everyone else. "There is definitely an electricity in the room."

Scales burned through Alisa's skin. Her fingers snapped as talons sprouted from the tips. Pain ricocheted through her as her dragon attempted to force a shift.

"Oh my gods," the witch cried. "Is she going to dragon out right here? She can't do that."

The room was tinged red.

"Alisa?" Even her mate calling to her seemed dull in her mind as Alisa tried to restrain her beast. There simply wasn't enough room for her to come out and play now.

A lasso of energy circled her, tightening by the second. Her dragon flailed, and Alisa flinched while she wriggled, trying to escape the magic.

It'd been an ambush—an attack. Declan had lulled her into a false sense of safety only to bring the witch to catch Alisa. This had all been a setup. Well, she wasn't about to go down without a fight.

With her talon-tipped fingers, Alisa launched herself past Declan, straight at the witch.

A bevy of wide eyes and stunned expressions greeted her. Just as the tip of her claw scratched the witch's cheek, a ball of flames pummeled into Alisa. It halted her forward trajectory and actually sent her flying backward, crashing into the seventy-five-inch television mounted to the wall.

"What the fuck?" Alisa couldn't be sure who'd said it.

"Alisa!" That was Declan.

Being a fire dragon herself, the fire merely heated her skin but burned the clothes from her body. Naked, with shards of television in her back, Alisa slid down the wall as a blast of cold filled the room.

Teal dragon scales covered Declan. His fists were balled, and a tail jutted from the bottom of his spine. Opposite him stood her half brother covered in maroon scales with smoke billowing from his nose. Tension was thick in the air. Water dripped from him and the ceiling. The witch, with icicles in her hair, cowered in a corner. The human was nowhere to be seen.

Alisa's beast, effectively restrained by the magical entanglement, couldn't fully come forward. It left Alisa in a state of half and half. Scales all over her body, large canines jutting down past her lips, and long claws tipping her fingers.

Wriggling against her binds, Alisa bared her teeth as she scrambled to her feet.

"What the hell is going on?" demanded her half brother.

While Alisa would've liked to know that too, she couldn't stick around and find out. The witch used powerful magic against her. Fire and ice had clashed. She didn't have time to question how two dragons, in mostly human form, were able to breathe their elements. That was something she'd have to sort through at another time. She had to escape. If for no other reason than to protect her egg.

With both hands covering her stomach, she darted past them with all the speed she could muster. Thankfully, she had the cloaking tattoo. Since she was in a partially shifted state, it would keep her hidden from humans as she ran through Manhattan.

Unfortunately, the bindings around her meant her dragon couldn't fully come forth. That left her apartment as the only place she could hide.

If her mate were true, he would know why she fled. He'd follow and find her to protect their egg. She didn't want to consider the alternative more than she already had. Fate gave him to her. She needed to trust that and him.

At this point, she didn't have any other choice. It wasn't about her own safety but what she carried. The only way to protect her young was to flee. So she did the only thing she could and ran.

34

DECLAN

It all happened so fast. Huffing, with his chest heaving, Declan's gaze darted around his apartment. He barely caught the flash of her as she raced out of his place.

"Alisa!" he shouted after her, but his friends blocked his path.

"What just happened?" Ella asked.

"How did you both do that?" Felicity interjected.

"Let me go!" Declan struggled against Gideon's hold. "I have to catch her."

"She tried to attack Felicity," his best friend said through gritted teeth. "And Ella."

"What the fuck was that about?" Ella chimed in.

Declan whirled with his fists clenched and his dragon teeth bared at his *former* friend. Definitely no longer friends after she cast some sort of spell over his mate—his mate who carried his egg! Felicity had to have done something to every one of the dragons in the room. They all seemed blocked from a full transition. What the hell was she thinking? Her inexperience showed.

"What did you do?" He charged toward her. "Explain this."

Declan held up his scale-covered hands. He was half-dragon. That never happened. Once a shift started, it didn't pause midway. It either receded or he went full beast. Never was he stuck somewhere between.

It had to have been magical intervention, and Felicity was the only spellcaster in the room.

Felicity's eyes widened, filled with fear, as she backed away from him. "Nothing! I swear." Again, her palms were toward him.

"Lies!" he bellowed as he tossed a burned stool out of the way.

"Calm down," Ella begged.

Declan twisted and lunged without thinking. How dare the human suggest such a ridiculous and impossible idea. His pregnant mate just fled. She'd been attacked by not only a witch but a dragon. Ella was out of her damn mind. A silly human would never understand.

A solid wall of muscle met his back. Gideon stood between them, and Declan bounced off his other *former* friend and landed square on his ass in a puddle of water.

Snarling, he got to his feet and threw a punch, connecting with Gideon's jaw and sending him sprawling back into Ella.

"Stop it!" Felicity shrieked.

"My mate!" Declan rumbled. "You breathed fire at my mate, and she is with egg."

"Egg?" the women repeated in unison.

Head down, arms out, Gideon charged toward Declan and speared him in the gut, knocking the wind out of him. The two men barreled into the living room area, tripping over the large ottoman and coffee table combination.

Gideon had the upper hand for mere seconds, sitting on top of Declan before Declan bucked his hips and threw his friend backward face-first into the couch.

"Stop it!" Felicity repeated in such a high-pitched tone both Declan and Gideon covered their ears.

When both men were pinned to the ground by unseeable hands, they growled. Declan's dragon had receded mostly but continued to roar in his ears. The beast flailed, trying to escape his human prison to chase after his mate.

"I agree." The older woman's voice sent chills down Declan's spine.

Immediately, his beast stilled within him. Gasps rang out from his friends.

"Auntie." It sounded like an accusation from Felicity. "What did you do?"

The older witch sauntered into Declan's apartment as though she owned the place. "As always, I did what I had to."

Declan fought furiously against whatever magic held him down.

Barely casting him a sideways glance, Josephine, the Ember Witch, snorted. "I warned you."

"This doesn't concern you," Felicity said.

"What have you done to them?" Ella demanded as she skittered over to Gideon's side.

Rolling her eyes, Josephine flicked her wrist. "I guess you could say I put them in time-out. They can't tear each other to pieces in an apartment building. Do you have any idea how hard it is to restrain *three* dragons? They would have brought the whole place down if the three of them shifted at once."

"Why are you here?" Felicity demanded.

"To protect you and all of us from the golden dragon."

"No one asked you to do that," Declan growled.

Josephine rolled her eyes. "Well, your judgment is obviously impaired. I should've picked up on it sooner, but I had only thought you two were sleeping together. I didn't realize what a horrible predicament you put yourself in."

"You're wrong," Declan spat.

Josephine folded her arms over her chest. "The fates are never wrong."

"I didn't say *they* were," he sneered. "I said *you* were."

She narrowed her eyes at him. "You don't challenge the voice of destiny."

"We are true mates, not by choice. Destiny brought us together. So, whatever bullshit about a curse you put on her and her family is nothing more than a petty vendetta."

Another round of gasps came from the women. "Fated mates?" Felicity repeated.

He hadn't gotten around to explaining all of that before Alisa came out of the shower and all hell broke loose.

"Impossible," the older witch snapped.

"Auntie, you can't go against fate. If Declan said destiny brought them together, then that's a fact. He wouldn't lie about anything like that."

Josephine's eye twitched. "He's incorrect. She's obviously convinced him—"

"You're the one who's wrong," Declan roared and somehow found the strength to push back against the invisible hold the elder witch had on him. Straining every muscle in his body, with his dragon's assistance, he got to his feet.

Fear flashed in her eyes.

"Release us," Declan demanded. "From whatever spell you have casted upon us. Whatever curse you have placed on Alisa is broken. Destiny blessed our union. It's time the guardians of fate did the same."

Josephine's nostrils flared. "Her mother orphaned Felicity's parents. She killed his sister." She pointed toward Gideon.

"My what?" he asked, slowly sitting up as whatever magical hold on them receded.

"Golden dragons bring pain and suffering. They're a menace. We have to rid them from the world."

"Alisa did none of those things." Declan stepped toward the older witch. "Free her."

"Who do *you* think you are making demands of *me*? An Ember Witch."

"I am her mate." Declan's dragon snapped his jaws, desperate to take a bite of the older woman.

"Children," she muttered. "You will never understand the severity of this. It is your life on the line. Hers." She pointed to Felicity. "And theirs." She moved her finger to Gideon and Ella.

"She will take every one of you down, even if she doesn't mean to. It is her destiny as a golden dragon to destroy everything she holds dear. I do not make the rules."

"Fate does."

Again, the older woman shook with what could only be rage. "You don't know what you're in for."

"You're blinded by hate." Declan stared her straight in the eyes. "It's corrupted your duty."

"Don't you dare talk to me about my duty." She jutted a finger at him.

"Auntie, he's right." Felicity approached Josephine cautiously. "If fate brought them together, you cannot break them apart."

"Watch me."

In a whirlwind, a tiny tornado appeared in his apartment. The force of the gales shoved everyone back. Gideon covered his mate protectively. Felicity and Declan were forced against opposite walls. Shards of television, water droplets, ash, pillows, papers, bits of magazine, and other apartment junk swirled in a circle.

When his apartment door slammed, everything crashed to the ground. The Ember Witch was gone. Destruction littered his apartment in her wake. Declan's heart was in his throat. His dragon clawed at the mental walls. They had to find Alisa before Josephine did.

35

ALISA

R unning as fast as her legs could carry her, Alisa finally made it to her apartment. In her current state, it was the only place to go. Slamming the door behind her, she leaned against it and slid down to the floor.

With her head against her knees, she panted, trying to catch her breath. The witch knew where she lived. She couldn't stay there long, but she couldn't think of anywhere else to come up with a plan.

The scales on her arms had flaked off on her run. Wriggling in her mind, her beast struggled against the binding the witch had spelled on her. She couldn't fully shift. It put her at a horrible disadvantage against any sort of magic. As a supernatural being, her best offense and defense was her beast. Without it, she'd be completely helpless. How was she supposed to protect her egg?

Sobs bubbled up in her throat before exploding from her. Crying wouldn't solve a damn thing, but she couldn't stop the waterworks. The full force of everything she'd endured since arriving in Manhattan had finally overwhelmed her.

She never felt good about trusting Declan's witch friend. Witches and golden dragons didn't mix. It didn't take long for his friend to prove that right. Now what was she supposed to do? Her mate had deceived her.

No. He couldn't. Something else had to have happened.

As the events replayed themselves in her mind over her dragon's snarls, her chest tightened, and her heart was just as restrained as her beast. How could he not—then it hit her.

He had.

Somehow, when fire flew from her half brother's half-human face, ice shot from her mate. He had protected her and their egg. Her head snapped up, and she blinked away the tears, sniffled, and swiped her nose with her arm.

In the kerfuffle, she hadn't processed everything that had gone on. Somehow, two males in half-dragon form had breathed their elements. That was supposed to be impossible. Not to mention Declan had done it to defend her.

He hadn't betrayed her.

Pushing up from her wallowing position, she got to her feet. Fate hadn't given her a bad mate. Her self-preservation overrode any sort of sense she had. She needed to go back. There would be no way she could defeat the Ember Witch by herself. Declan had to be by her side.

Shoulders square, spine straight, head held high, and tears gone, Alisa marched to her bedroom. She couldn't traipse around New York in the nude. With her dragon fully imprisoned inside her, she wouldn't have to worry about losing her clothes.

Tugging the drawers open, she rummaged through, finding a sports bra, panties, and comfortable clothes. Once dressed, she was ready to join forces with her mate and go to battle. If his friends stood with them, so be it. If they didn't, fuck them.

They couldn't deny fate any more than the Ember Witch.

She wouldn't surrender.

Her hand covered her belly. Their egg needed them to win this war. Her entire line of golden dragons deserved for her to defeat the Ember Witch. Destiny had taken its stance when it blessed her with Declan. Now it was her turn to fight for it. With her mate standing with her, there was nothing they couldn't do.

With her hand on the doorknob, she twisted it, filled with resolve. Hope swirled in her gut as though it cradled the egg growing inside her. She had fate on her side.

One quick pull and the door opened.

She gasped.

Standing in the hallway of her apartment, with worry creasing her features, was her grandmother. With a deep inhale, her face brightened. "Thank the gods," she said as she stepped forward and wrapped Alisa in a tight hug.

"What are you doing here?" Alisa asked.

"The magical energy swirling around this city has my dragon on edge. Is it always like this?" Her grandmother released her and moved into the apartment.

"Not really, no." Alisa didn't have time for a visit. "I already told you. You can't stop me from going against the witch."

Turning to face Alisa, a tight-lipped frown marred her grandmother's features. "I am aware."

Her mouth opened to say more but quickly closed. The older woman's brows furrowed, and her gaze fell to Alisa's belly. It flicked back and forth between her stomach and face several times before her grandmother covered her mouth.

She could either smell it or sense it. Either way, she knew.

Alisa placed a hand on her abdomen and nodded. "I am with egg." She didn't have to, but she needed to affirm it. Also, it wasn't the first occasion she'd actually verbalized it.

It felt good to say.

"But, but, but," her grandmother stammered before she raced forward and placed her own hands on Alisa. "The curse."

Blossoming pride bloomed in Alisa's chest. "Declan and I have defied it. Fate smiled upon us. We are not only mated, but we have made another dragon. Which is why we have to fight now. It's not just about us anymore."

Tears dripped down her grandmother's cheeks. A smile spread from her lips. "Forgiven."

The single word slipping from her lips was filled with hope. It fed Alisa's own.

"Almost." Alisa frowned. "We need to remind the witches who they serve—fate and not their own interests. Though, I'm not sure it's all the witches or just this one Ember Witch." She pursed her lips, contemplating that for a moment.

Her grandma wrung her hands with her gaze locked on Alisa, waiting for something.

"I don't know how, but I need my mate by my side to do it." It was all Alisa had.

"And where is he?" Her grandmother glanced around the apartment, seeking him.

Alisa rubbed the back of her neck. "I'm on my way to get him now." No need to let her grandmother in on how she'd sort of abandoned him with a witch. Minor detail. Besides, she'd only done what was best for their egg. She'd gotten away from the threat—the witch.

Her grandmother nodded slowly. "I'm going with you."

Alisa's gut urged her to deny the assistance. Her grandmother would turn into an obstacle. But she could use all the help she could get. The Ember Witch had an entire coven behind her. Alisa could have her mate and grandmother.

Three dragons were better than two.

36

DECLAN

Despite Declan's dragon struggling inside his mind, Josephine's spell restrained it. He couldn't shift. Scales dropped from his skin and *tinked* as they landed on the tile floor. He shook his head and flailed his arms in an attempt to free his beast.

Nothing.

He glanced at his friend.

With his eyes squeezed tight, Gideon gritted his teeth. His fists were balled and the veins in his neck strained.

Nothing.

"She's bound you," Felicity said in a soft voice barely above a whisper.

"What does that mean?" Ella asked as she placed her hand on Gideon's shoulder. Concern laced her words and was written in her features.

Declan swallowed. "We're stuck as humans."

That would make their battle that much harder. She'd hobbled them with one spell before they even started.

"Why would she do that?" Ella peered between the three of them.

As a human, she had only the slightest grasp of all things supernatural. She'd only just learned of their existence. So these intricacies of magic definitely escaped her. Declan didn't have the time to explain.

Felicity hugged herself. Her frown seemed as though she carried quite the heavy burden. "My aunt is defying her purpose. As an Ember Witch, she has to protect fate.

She isn't supposed to go against it. It's always been her excuse for whatever she's done. But this, whatever her problem is, it's defying her calling."

"What does that mean for us?" Declan asked. "Alisa is with egg."

He had to find her. In her condition, she shouldn't be alone.

"You really need to explain that," Ella commented.

"She's pregnant," Gideon whispered. "We'll talk about it later. It's not something we can get into right now."

"Holy shit," Ella's eyes widened. "With an egg?"

"The coven will not approve of what she's doing." Felicity had a far-off look in her eyes.

Declan didn't have time for everyone to have an existential crisis right now. A witch was after his mate, and it wasn't any old witch. An Ember Witch had it in for Alisa and his egg. He couldn't stand there chatting about it.

Shaking his head, he forewent answers and left to find her. They were stronger together. She wouldn't stand a chance against Josephine without him. He didn't know where to even start looking for her, but his dragon would.

The beast had always found her. He suspected through their bond. They were mates, drawn to each other on every level. He'd locate her the old-fashioned way. Even if his dragon was stuck inside him. The animal snarled in agreement as he charged toward the door.

"Where are you going?" his three friends called in unison.

"To find and protect my mate. In case you all forgot, there is a rogue Ember Witch after her. I kind of need to address that." He wrenched open the door, aware each second he wasted was more risk for Alisa and their egg.

"You can't go alone." Felicity chased him out the door, with Gideon and Ella not far behind.

"I'd prefer not to, but can I trust where your loyalties lie?"

"What's that supposed to mean?" Felicity countered.

Declan whirled and glared down at her. "You're a witch in a coven."

She balked and folded her arms over her chest. "My aunt is going against the coven right now. If they knew—"

"Then go tell them," Declan growled. He didn't have time for witch politics.

Scales beneath his skin grated over one another. A chill ran through him. His dragon raged within him. The beast wasn't tolerating being restrained well. He wanted release to taste vengeance. Unfortunately, Josephine was powerful. So, the only way to free his dragon was to solve this issue with her.

Gritting his teeth, he trotted down the stairs and headed out of the building. The thudding of their footsteps behind him meant his friends were right on his heels. While he wasn't sure how, he knew they would stand behind him and help.

A witch, a human, and three dragons were better than just the two of them facing Josephine alone. They needed all the support they could get.

While he may have questioned Felicity's loyalty, he'd done it more as a test than anything else. He'd witnessed her stand up to her aunt with his own eyes, but if she was conflicted at all, even the slightest bit, he needed to know that now before anything big happened.

His mate and his egg were at stake. He couldn't take any chances.

Now all they had to do was find Alisa and...

Yeah, then what?

He'd figure that out when the time came. The first step was to connect with his mate. Everything else could and would sort itself out afterward. He had to find her before Josephine did.

His heart jumped to his throat. Flicking his tail and clawing at the walls, his dragon fought what held him inside Declan. Josephine couldn't get to Alisa first. He had to. She wouldn't stand a chance against the elder witch alone.

Urgency coursed through his veins as he hit the pavement outside his apartment building.

Where would Alisa go?

Closing his eyes, he lifted his chin. Sniffing the air, he sought her scent to follow it.

"What's he doing?" Ella whispered.

"Probably trying to smell her," Gideon answered softly. "It's something we can do."

Declan wasn't a bloodhound, but he was a shifter. He had advanced senses, and he needed this one the most right now. All he had to do was catch a whiff of her.

"You can *smell* me?" Ella paused. "From, like, far away?"

Gideon chuckled. "Yes. Don't worry. You're divine."

"I don't know how I feel about that."

37

ALISA

Alisa wasn't sure where they'd go as they descended the stairs toward the lobby of her apartment building, but she had faith that her dragon would find Declan. His apartment wasn't safe. After all the magic, fire, and ice nonsense, she wouldn't go back there without being certain the witch was dealt with. Either way, they'd have to hide somewhere while they planned how to effectively deal with the Ember Witch.

"Do witches even have weaknesses?" she muttered as they got to the final landing.

"Well, they can't heal like we can. They aren't as strong as we are. They are mortal," her grandmother rattled off basic information. "But Ember Witches are a completely different breed. They're more powerful and can do stuff others can't."

Shaking her head, Alisa said, "So, basically we're screwed."

"I tried to warn you."

"That's not helpful."

At the last step, her grandmother turned to her. "Lee, if I knew how to defeat this bitch, I would've done it to save your mother or your grandfather or..."

When she trailed off, Alisa peered at her. However, before she could question it, the door to her building opened and drew her attention away. Shifting her gaze over her grandmother's head, her body stiffened, and her dragon went on high alert—not that she could do a damn thing. The witch had imprisoned her.

"Oh good, you're here," Duncan said as he rubbed his hands together.

He couldn't have picked a worse occasion to show up. Alisa couldn't deal with him right now. There was too much at stake to sift through their familial baggage.

"I probably should give you some space, but then again, I've done that your entire life—"

"You have a lot of nerve showing up here," her grandmother snarled as she waved her finger.

"Grandma," Alisa admonished.

She didn't need a showdown between those two. It may have brewed for thirty-plus years, but they'd just have to shelve it for now.

Ignoring Alisa, her grandmother continued slowly toward the man. "Do you have any idea what her coming here to find *you* has done?"

He furrowed his brows as he glanced between Alisa and her grandmother. "Lillian?"

Alisa scrambled to get around her grandmother. Smoke trailed out of her grandma's nostrils as she put her hands on her hips. Alisa needed to defuse this before they exploded in the lobby.

"We can't do this right now," she reminded her grandma as she positioned herself between them.

"It should have been you!" Her grandmother bumped into Alisa as she glared daggers at Duncan.

Glancing over her shoulder, Alisa caught his wounded look. What the hell was she supposed to do?

Gripping her grandmother's shoulders, Alisa tried to get her to focus. "Grandma!"

"Vivienne went insane and did what she did because of *you*!" Tears streamed down her grandmother's face. "It should've been *you*. Now it's going to be *your daughter*. When are you going to take responsibility?"

"Dad?" Gideon's voice startled everyone.

Alisa and Duncan turned to see Declan and his friends entering the lobby.

Relief washed over Alisa. Her mate was there. Her dragon pushed her to go to him, but she knew better than to step from between Duncan and her grandmother.

Duncan's shoulders slumped. He opened his mouth, but Alisa cut him off. "The longer we're out in the open, the easier it will be to be found. And none of us want that."

Alisa sought Declan's gaze as he shuffled past his friends to go to her side. "We don't have a plan," he whispered into her ear as though most of the group wouldn't be able to hear him.

She pressed her fingers to her temples. "I am aware."

What she wouldn't give to have the faintest idea how to win this battle. She leaned into him, seeking the slightest sense of solace or support. When he draped his arm over her and pulled her tighter against him, it eased some of the stress but not enough.

"I'm sorry, but who is searching for you?" Duncan asked.

"Why are you here?" Gideon asked as he came around, keeping Ella at his back.

"There is so much to explain," Alisa offered. "And we just can't do it now."

"You know damn well who is out to get them." Her grandmother gestured toward Declan and Alisa.

Duncan's gaze flicked back and forth between Alisa, Declan, and her grandmother.

"I'm sorry. I understand we're like in urgency mode here, but I distinctly heard that lady there"—Gideon pointed to Alisa's grandmother—"say something about daughter. If we could just—"

"I have fathered another besides you and your brother," Duncan said, sounding exasperated. "Meet your sister, Alisa."

Declan and Gideon's eyes widened, and their mouths hung agape.

"This is like the craziest soap opera ever," Ella commented.

Alisa stepped away from her shocked mate and waved her hands. "Okay, seriously. Lives are on the line here." Namely hers, Declan's, and their egg's. Maybe her grandmother's too. "We can't stand around talking family trees. We need to go somewhere else, like a safe house or something. Somewhere she can't get in." And live there apparently. Because Alisa didn't have any other ideas.

"What about the fabrication room at Arach?" Gideon suggested. "It's pretty locked down. There are a bazillion fire protocols because we melt metal. I'm pretty sure it's reinforced. There's a singular entrance and one exit."

"She's magical. Can't she just appear anywhere she wants?" Ella asked.

Felicity shook her head. "No. Magic doesn't work that way. We don't teleport, but we ride the wind, sort of."

Alisa's budding headache throbbed against her skull. "What does that mean?"

"Witches, even Ember Witches, can't evaporate and manifest somewhere else. If a breeze can get there, so can a witch, but it's a complicated spell. So, not everyone can do it."

"Isn't your aunt like the queen witch?" Ella asked.

Witches had queens? Alisa didn't know about the politics of witches.

The younger witch frowned and stuttered slightly, as though she couldn't find the right words. "No. We don't have a monarchy. We have a coven. Our coven still answers to the Council of Others. Though I think Auntie Josephine sits on it."

"Take my car," Duncan ordered. "Justin will drive you to Arach. Gideon is right. The fabrication room will offer the best protection, and if nothing else, it will buy you time. She'd never know to look for you there."

Declan nodded and slid his arm around Alisa. "Let's go."

"Grandma." Alisa turned. "You have to come too. She is out for all golden dragons. I wouldn't put it past her to go for you if she can't get me."

Her grandmother inhaled deeply and lifted her chin as she went to Alisa's side.

"We'll hang back here and see if she shows up," Felicity offered. "Maybe I can talk some sense into her."

Duncan shook his head. But it was Alisa's grandmother who spoke. "There is nothing left to be said. Josephine is bitter. This goes back farther than you know."

"Then we stay as a group." Gideon nodded.

"I've already called an Uber," Ella chimed in. "We'll be right behind Justin."

As Declan ushered her out of the building, Alisa wasn't sure if she should find solace in the group rallying around her or not. Yes, more forces were better, but they were against the ultimate enemy. Would it even matter facing off such an elder Ember Witch? By finding Declan, had she doomed herself and her egg?

Tears welled in her eyes. Grabbing his arm, she stopped moving.

Declan scanned her features.

"Can we do this?" she asked. "Is there any hope that we can somehow end the hex?"

"The curse is already broken." He squeezed her hands. "We have an egg on the way. Now, we just have to convince the witch."

"But is that even possible? How are we supposed to do that?"

"Fate will find a way."

38

DECLAN

Never in the world of silences had there been one as heavy as the quiet in the car on the way to the Arach building. With Alisa tucked against Declan's side, he rubbed her shoulder absentmindedly and stared off at nothing. Perhaps he should've enjoyed it. From what he'd seen so far, Josephine intended to bring a hell of a lot of chaos their way. This calm before the storm wouldn't last.

Where was she anyway?

If she were truly seeking Alisa, why hadn't she started at her apartment? That's where he'd gone. Okay, he used his dragon to find her. He actually hadn't known where to look without his beast. Alisa said the witch had already shown up at her place. Maybe that's why she didn't go there.

Maybe the safest location to hide out for now *was* her apartment. Hide in the most obvious place and perhaps the witch would overlook it.

Shaking his head, he pinched the bridge of his nose. It wasn't worth the risk. Pain spiked through his brain, and for once, it wasn't his inner animal. Though, the beast continued to battle against his magical constraints. Knowing he couldn't shift if he wanted to made his skin itch. That would get old real fast. He was already over it.

It didn't take long for Justin, the mongoose shifter driver, to pull up to their destination. So much for their reprieve.

Before Justin could exit the car, Alisa's grandmother flung her door open and jumped out. Declan took that half a second of privacy before Justin opened Alisa's door to give her a squeeze.

"We got this." He did his best to reassure her. Though admittedly, it was a weak attempt.

To her credit, she tipped her chin up to him and offered him a strained smile. "We have no other choice."

Fair. With the two of them staring down a metaphorical, and inevitable, barrel of a gun, a positive outlook, no matter how forced, was the only thing keeping them going. If they admitted to themselves it was hopeless, they might as well just roll over and wait for Josephine to end their lives.

That wasn't what Declan wanted. If he had to put on a fake smile and a brave face, so be it. He would fight. That bitch would have to take him out swinging. This was his mate and his egg. He might not have expected this to happen to him at twenty-five, but this was his destiny. He'd be damned if he'd let Alisa and his hatchling down.

"How do we tip him?" Alisa's grandmother whispered after they'd gotten out of the car. "Is it an app or something? I don't have my phone with me."

Alisa half chuckled. "He's a personal driver. You don't tip him."

The displaced moment of normalcy was refreshing.

Justin seemed to stifle a smile. "Have a good afternoon." He dipped his chin and climbed back into the driver's seat.

One day, Declan would find out what Justin did with his time when he wasn't carting Gideon's family around. Did he have other duties? Or did they pay him to just sit in the car all day? He seemed to be on-call twenty-four seven.

Taking a deep breath, he pushed the pointless tangent out of his mind. There was a threat about, and his dragon was already thrashing inside him on high alert. He needed to be vigilant.

Another car pulled up behind Justin's. The large white SUV's door opened, and Declan's friends spilled out. Gideon, Ella, and then Felicity from the back. Duncan had ridden in the front. He stood with his head high as he buttoned the jacket to his designer suit.

It was subtle, but Declan caught the slight flare of Duncan's nostrils. Declan did the same—scenting the air. He couldn't remember what the witch smelled like, but he hoped he'd recognize it.

Her spell made his skin crawl, so he couldn't rely on sensing her magical presence. She had put them behind the eight ball.

How long could this incantation last? A fresh wave of fear tightened in his chest. Could it be permanent? That'd most definitely drive them all mad.

Which seemed to be Josephine's goal. Maybe she played the long game. This was her punishment for them. This was the curse. She'd keep them restrained like this, unable to access their dragons, until they went insane.

Then she'd appear when they'd finally lost their minds and finish the job. Damn, he hated the unknown.

"Let's get inside before she spots us," Duncan said as he glanced up and down the street.

Nodding, Declan placed his hand on the small of Alisa's back to usher her toward the building.

"This seems off," his mate commented. "She should've shown herself by now."

"This is the safest option. She knows the history," Duncan asserted. "She would never expect me to help. Not after what happened."

Declan kept his suspicions to himself. There was no need to air that horrendous thought to the group. They had no defense for it.

"She wants us to be lulled into a false sense of security," Alisa's grandmother offered. "I am familiar with Josephine. She is meticulous. I wouldn't put it past her to be watching us squirm in the distance."

Ah, hell. Everything Alisa's grandmother said made his theory that much more plausible. How were they supposed to combat that?

Immediately, Alisa glanced over her shoulder and scanned the busy Manhattan street. "I don't like it."

"Me either," Declan agreed as he reached for the door. "But we have to take the opportunity to try to get one step ahead of her if we can."

"It's the only idea we have," Gideon offered. "We might as well go with it until something better comes up."

Despite the unseasonably warm temperatures, a chill ran down Declan's spine. The thick essence of foreboding energy felt like static. Every little thing had his gaze darting this way and that. He couldn't exist like this—*they* couldn't.

He needed to end the threat. There would be no peace while Josephine roamed the Earth.

"You know this is going to be extra difficult because she has a seat on the Council of Others." Felicity mentioned the governing body of all supernatural kind as they entered the building.

"It doesn't change that what she's done, and is doing, is wrong," Declan asserted.

"I agree," Felicity said with her head down as she texted feverishly on her phone. Who the hell was she talking to at a time like this?

"I'm not sure what will be worse, the wrath of the Ember Witch or the Council of Others." The defeat in Alisa's voice wouldn't do.

"Both are severe," Duncan commented. "Just in different ways. I wouldn't want to be on the bad side of either..." He cleared his throat. "Sorry."

"You should be," Alisa's grandmother snapped.

"I really need you two to stop." Alisa pressed her fingers to her temples. "We will never get through this if you keep bickering."

The elders of the group exchanged glances. Something passed between them, but Declan couldn't be sure. He needed to redirect the energy.

"The Council will understand." He tried to sound resolute in his proclamation. Far too many layers complicated all of this.

"I hope so," Alisa said before biting her lips together and squeezing his hand.

The group stopped at the elevator, allowing Duncan to take the lead. It was his building, after all. After the ding, the merry band of misfits shuffled into the elevator. Ladies first. Once inside, after inserting his key card, Duncan pressed the button for the basement level.

Declan had never been down that way. His time in the building was limited to a few days a month in conference rooms. He preferred to work from home. Gideon practically lived there. At least one of them was familiar with the layout.

Shifting his weight from foot to foot, Declan did his best to keep his nervous fidgets to a minimum. Everyone was on edge. There was no need to make it worse by annoying everyone in the tight space.

How long was this stupid ride to the basement anyway? Was it a subbasement or something?

An image of a dark cave-like lair popped into his head. On any other occasion, he might have been amused by such a thing but not today. He shoved it out of his mind. *Focus.*

Finally, the elevator dinged, and the doors slid open.

Like a giant exhale, they spilled out of the elevator, thankful for the space. Scanning the tables, shelving, kilns, and smelting equipment, Declan positioned himself in front of Alisa.

The doors closed behind them as they fanned out. "I'll clear a space so we can all sit and plan our attack," Ella offered.

As a human, she had little to bring to the table in the way of defense, so this would have to do. She probably should've stayed home. Humans had no business in the middle of supernatural creatures' affairs, but she was Gideon's mate. If Declan wanted him at his side, he'd have to deal with Ella.

"So nice of you to finally show up."

Collectively, the group froze.

39

ALISA

While Alisa wasn't crazy familiar with the Ember Bitch, she knew her voice. It wasn't every day someone threatened her. So, she'd taken note when that wench had.

Declan immediately shoved her behind him, holding on to her upper arm with a viselike grip as scales erupted over his skin. Alisa's inner beast slammed against the mental and magical barriers holding her inside. Shifting was impossible, so there was no use in trying. If only her dragon understood.

A thick, electric blue and azure bolt shot forward out of her mate. *Ice.* He breathed ice. Half-human, half-dragon, he could tap into his element. Insane but useful. They weren't completely powerless.

Fire followed the ice, directed toward the witch. Gideon, with his mate tucked safely behind him, had used his element to defend her. If Alisa's heart wasn't threatening to explode from her chest, she might have been touched by her half brother's gesture to protect her.

To her right, her grandmother roared. Turning toward the sound, Alisa gasped. Was the room big enough? She looked up, down, left, and right. Vaulted ceilings. Thank all the gods.

Popping and grunting drew her attention. Her father and grandmother shifted into their massive dragon forms. Though hunched, the several-ton beings both screeched while stretching their long necks toward the Ember Witch. The sound practically deafened Alisa.

Hopefully, this room was more than just fireproof. Soundproof would be really help-ful right now. If they survived this encounter, she didn't need the wrath of the Council of Others for exposing humans to shifters and witches. The penalty for that would be worse than anything this witch had planned for them, for sure.

When the flurry of movement died, Alisa glanced around. One teal dragon, one ma-roon, both half-shifted. Check. A golden dragon to her right and a black beast to her left. That would definitely help with defenses. A human, not cowering, kudos to her, held her mate's shoulders. Lastly, a young witch. Okay, everyone present and accounted for.

Felicity stared straight ahead with her jaw locked. Her hands, balled into fists, had a hint of a yellow aura around them. Magic swirled in the air as she took purposeful steps forward.

Swallowing hard, Alisa watched the young woman push her way through the line of dragons, defending them. "Auntie," she called.

Alisa's gaze darted to the witch threatening them.

It was like they'd done nothing. Not a stitch of her clothing was singed from the fire Gideon had breathed. Her hair hung in a pair of plaits over her shoulders. There wasn't any indication that any frost or ice had touched her. How was that possible?

Wearing an expression filled with annoyance, she planted her hands on her hips. "You are on the wrong side, child."

Felicity shook her head. "I've spoken with the Council."

So that was who she'd been texting.

The older witch's eye twitched.

"Divina isn't pleased with what you've done."

Alisa didn't know who that was, but she assumed she sat on the council or something. Why else would Felicity mention her? Oh! Maybe she was in the coven too.

"She's young," Josephine quipped. "Step aside so I can end this mistake." A green aura pulsed around the elder. That wasn't good.

Alisa's mouth ran dry as she clung to Declan. Her dragon raged inside her, desperate to join the fight. The magical restraint wouldn't allow it. She'd been rendered just as useless in this face-off as Gideon's human mate. Alisa had no choice but to sit back and watch a young witch fight an elder witch on her behalf.

The odds weren't in her favor.

"How no one noticed your genocide—"

Josephine scoffed. "Genocide? Don't be dramatic. There are plenty of dragons. This particular breed is detrimental to everyone. They are dangerous. My actions are to protect all of us—magical and shifter alike."

Alisa barely noticed the sound of scales flaking and hitting the ground. Against her better judgment, she turned to witness her grandmother's dragon receding. Why would she morph back into her human form? She could do much more damage as a dragon than she could as a human. She didn't have to breathe fire to help. Her size alone was her advantage.

"You need to be honest with them, Jo, and yourself." Her grandmother surprised everyone as she spoke, rather familiarly, and moved to stand beside the younger witch.

Josephine scowled. Her hands shot forward as yellow bolts danced through the air toward Alisa's grandmother.

Alisa gasped and attempted to push past Declan. He was immovable.

A wall of blue, almost like a bubble, surrounded her grandmother and Felicity before the magic shocks struck them. Felicity had protected her grandmother.

"Get out of the way," Josephine spat. "Don't you see? This is what they do. They're putting you in danger."

"*You're* the threat. Not them," Felicity retorted. "They just want to live."

"They killed *your* parents." She turned her ire to Duncan. "And cracked *your* egg."

"You murdered my mom," Alisa shouted back.

Josephine's attention shot to Alisa and a chill ran down her spine. She should've stayed quiet. Though unlikely, there was a tiny portion of her that had hoped the woman had forgotten she was there.

"I wouldn't have had to if she hadn't gone after my coven," the older witch sneered.

"If you hadn't meddled with mates, this all could've been avoided," Alisa's grandmother announced. "No one would've died. Thomas could still be here."

The Ember Witch shook with rage. "He. Was. Mine."

"Fate said otherwise." The sadness in her grandma's tone pierced Alisa's heart.

There was so much pain, but who the hell was Thomas?

"Don't you think one hundred twenty-seven years is long enough? Let the pain go. You've made so many suffer. It has to stop."

Holy fucking shit.

"How is that even possible?" Ella's blurted whisper echoed Alisa's own sentiments.

Witches were not immortal. Because of their ability to heal, shifters had extended lifespans, and living well into their three hundreds was possible, but not a witch. That seemed like a really long-ass time for something so close to human.

"You don't *know* suffering," the witch's voice quaked.

"Fate gave him to *me*." Alisa's grandmother's voice cracked harder.

"Yet you had the audacity to take another." Josephine hissed and narrowed her eyes. "He couldn't have been your fated mate if you did that."

Wait, what? Alisa couldn't believe her ears. Her grandmother had a fated mate before her grandfather? How old was she anyway? Alisa had never thought to ask.

"As much as you say you are the guardian of fate, you sure don't understand it." Her grandmother hung her head. "She is far more forgiving than you give her credit for. Happiness is the goal of destiny."

"You only get one. And you stole mine." Again, bolts of yellow energy charged toward Alisa's grandmother. "You brought this on your kind. You deserved to suffer. Then your daughter only confirmed it. Your sin transcended generations."

Felicity shot back with the blue ones, cutting them off at the pass. "Are you serious right now? All of this is over a man?"

One. Two. Three. The younger witch countered each blast from the older one. If it were under any other circumstances, Alisa would've been impressed. Except her life was on the line, so she wallowed in her anxiety as the witches battled.

"You will never understand until fate blesses you with a mate, Felicity," the Ember Witch said. "Thomas was my gift."

"You chose him. Fate didn't," Alisa's grandmother implored. "If it had been destiny, he never would've heard my call."

"He wasn't even a dragon," Josephine screeched before hurling another barrage of energy.

Blood trickled from Felicity's nose as she held out both palms, attempting to block the massive ball coming at them. Using that much magic must have drained her. It wasn't infinite. When she struggled to hold off the attack, Duncan's long black tail flung in that direction. He swatted it away as though it were baseball.

Another large torched flame shot forward, aimed at the Ember Witch. She let out an exasperated cry, and the wall of flames turned around. An ice wall formed as Declan sprayed his element to block the inferno headed toward them.

"This needs to stop," Alisa's grandmother announced. "I'm the reason this started. Take me and end it."

"What?" everyone else in the room said in unison.

The Ember Witch cocked her head to the side as she eyed Alisa's grandmother warily.

"You can have my life's essence. Extend yours. I will give it to you, but only if you promise to end your vendetta. It began with us. Let it die with me. I'll shoulder the responsibility. Leave my granddaughter and her mate alone. Let their line continue with no prejudice from you or your coven, and you can have it. Guardian, let fate run its course and claim your peace."

40

Declan

"Grandma?" Alisa tried to step past Declan, but he'd be damned if he'd allow her get into the line of fire.

Josephine was unstable and couldn't be trusted. He'd never let Alisa step into danger. They had to wait and see what the older ones would do.

"What does that mean?" Ella asked in a whisper.

"I'll tell you later," Gideon hushed her.

Offering her essence to the witch was a tremendous sacrifice. Rumor had it, the Ember Witches lived so long because they could syphon energy from other supernatural beings. It was what, supposedly, made them so powerful. But he'd always dismissed that as too far-fetched.

Apparently not.

"You'd do that?" the old witch asked. "After all these years?"

"Too many have suffered."

"Why now?"

Alisa's grandmother glanced over her shoulder. Tenderness creased her features and even a warm smile spread across her lips. Affection, in the purest form, radiated off her as she looked at Alisa.

This entire issue, which had gone on for more than a century, was between these two women. He wasn't sure how many had suffered in the wake of their fallout, but he agreed it was time for it to end.

"Don't," Alisa pleaded. "There has to be another way."

Alisa's grandmother closed her eyes and shook her head slowly before returning her focus to the Ember Witch. "I've lived a lifetime and then some. I had happiness, even if it was fleeting. You deserve a chance at it."

She took two steps forward and lowered to her knees under the ire-filled glare of Josephine.

"I will never understand fate. Destiny played a cruel game with us, but I am ready to submit. I will sacrifice myself for my granddaughter and the future of golden dragons. Do you accept these terms?"

"No!" Alisa screamed again, trying to push past Declan.

Her pain throttled through him, but he had to hold her back.

"I fear it's the only way," he admitted. "She won't stop, and this is our egg's last hope."

Tears streamed down his mate's face. She continued to fight him. "Anything else. There has to be another way."

He kept his grip firm. This wasn't a pain he wished on anyone. His friends circled them but kept their distance. Their support was palpable.

Duncan had morphed back into a human and stood off to the side in stoic silence. The fact he was Alisa's father and Gideon was her half brother still hadn't officially sunk in, but this wasn't the time to process.

"Will you accept my penance for my sins?" Alisa's grandmother asked.

Josephine's nostrils flared, but she kept her attention down on the older dragon shifter.

"This is too extreme," Felicity mumbled. "Auntie, you can't do this. It goes against our coven."

The older witch flicked her attention to Felicity. "It is the lifeblood of our coven. The Ember Witches have practiced this since its inception. It is reserved for the most egregious of crimes."

"And this whole situation does not rise to that level." Felicity waved her hand outward in a circle. "It is the antithesis of our vows."

"She is responsible for the death of your parents. Yes, not by her hand, but it was her daughter, which she conceived against fate's wishes with a chosen mate. That is blasphemous."

Felicity balked. "You're wrong."

"Destiny chooses your partner. Not you."

"Times have changed."

The older witch scoffed and lowered her gaze. "One day, Felicity, you will understand."

"I'll tell the coven."

Josephine's chest expanded before she let out a heavy breath. "Some things are beyond even the Ember Witch Coven." Before anyone could rebut her point, the older witch lowered her attention back to Alisa's grandmother. She dipped her chin. "I accept your terms. Your line and all golden dragons are forgiven for your sins."

"No!" The pained shrieks rang out in unison from both Alisa and Felicity.

A plume of smoke swirled around the two older women. It was so thick they quickly disappeared from sight. Declan fought hard to keep Alisa by his side.

"I can feel your pain, but you can't stop it. This is between them. You have to let it happen," Declan whispered.

"Grandma!" Alisa screamed as she flailed futilely, trying to escape.

As the smoke dissipated, his mate fell against him. The witch and the older dragon were gone. With them went the magical restraints holding his dragon in. If he wanted to, he could shift. Not that there was a point.

The static of magic, which had charged the air since their arrival, fled with them. An eerie calm, laced with loss, filled the room. As Alisa sobbed into his chest, he held her tight, with one hand around her waist and the other cupping the back of her head.

"I have no family."

"You have a father." Duncan approached.

She peered up at him and sniffled. With red-rimmed, swollen eyes, she studied him.

"I may have missed the first thirty years, but if you'll let me, I will be involved in the next."

"You have a brother," Gideon offered. "Two actually. I'm pretty sure Fletcher will get on board once he finds out we have a sister."

Tears still spilling down her cheeks, she glanced in Felicity's direction. Her throat bobbed as she swallowed.

"I'll be a sister, if you'll let me," Ella said sheepishly. "I may not be a dragon, but I'm pretty cool."

Felicity sidled up beside her human friend. "Me too."

Duncan nodded.

Alisa took a deep breath as her gaze drifted from one to the other before lifting her eyes to meet Declan's.

The words his friends had spoken made his heart swell. This was what he'd envisioned his mating would be like—sort of. He'd always hoped, or expected, his circle to accept her—to love her and support her as he would. Never in his wildest imagination had he conjured this scenario, but he'd never questioned fate. This was the path they walked. They were the end of a curse that never should've been. Now it was time to focus on their future.

Running his index finger down her cheek, he swiped some of her tears away. "I'm *your* family. Our egg is *our* family. It's over. You're free. And you will always have family around you."

EPILOGUE

Declan

"I really like this one," Alisa said, holding up a mint-green newborn-sized pillowy comforter. "It's gender neutral and the softest thing I've ever felt."

Closing her eyes, she rubbed the blanket against her cheek as though to confirm it. Declan was surprised her cheeks weren't raw from all the items she'd tested with them. When she seemed satisfied with her choice, she refolded it.

"It's lovely," he commented from behind her. "But that's the fifth one you said you liked."

"Na-uh," Alisa retorted before placing it on the stack in the round bassinet.

Groaning, he flopped onto the bed. "Don't make me count them."

Their egg was due any day, and nesting had become her entire focus. Diapers, clothes, shoes, blankets, stuffies, lotions, bottles. They had baby supplies stacked everywhere in Declan's apartment. Maneuvering around inside his one bedroom took some planning. There was essentially an aisle to get around.

He couldn't stretch out anymore. Every inch of space was eaten up by something needed for the baby. To be fair, half of it was meant for their new mountain address in Upstate New York, but they hadn't had the opportunity to move anything yet.

They just kept collecting.

Alisa swore she'd get it all cleaned up in time for the hatching. Declan wasn't so sure. The clock still ticked, and she'd lay that egg soon.

He'd never been a hoarder before, so this situation was brand new to him. Alisa promised it was her hormones. He had no choice but to give her the benefit of the doubt. Instincts were a bitch, especially for pregnant shifters.

"Don't be such a curmudgeon," his mother, Sonya, nearly sang as she entered the room with an armload of bags. "I had at least fifteen blankets in your nest to keep you nice and toasty."

"If you bring another one into this apartment, so help me," Declan threatened.

Sonya chuckled. "I don't have any this time."

When her gaze caught Alisa's, she winked. There were definitely some in those bags. Squealing, Alisa headed toward Sonya with her hands out, making a grabby motion.

Declan rolled his eyes. What did one tiny dragon baby need with so many? For the love of the gods, Alisa was a fire dragon. Which meant their baby would most likely be fire as well and therefore wouldn't ever be cold! This was out of hand.

"Muslin wraps aren't blankets. They are swaddles."

"Seriously? Semantics?" Declan slapped his hand to his forehead. "We don't need a blanket for every day the egg sits in the nest. You know that, right?"

"Your opinion on this matter is neither desired nor required," Alisa joked as she pulled one swaddle blanket out after the other.

Large, seemingly soft, squares of thin fabric came from the bag. There seemed to be an endless supply. Had his mother bought every one in the store? Were there any left on the island of Manhattan?

"This," Sonya began, holding up a colorful piece of fabric. "Isn't for swaddling, it's for baby-wearing. I'll show you."

"We really don't have time for this." Declan sighed as he checked his phone for the time. "We're going to be late for dinner with the Hayes."

"That's tonight?" His mother frowned. "Are you sure you should gallivant around the city so close to her lay date?"

Declan lifted himself from the bed and shrugged. "I'm sure it will be fine."

In all honesty, he hadn't a clue if it was a good idea or not. The clutter in his apartment had him claustrophobic. He couldn't spend another hour in there before he'd flip his lid. This couldn't be healthy for any of them.

He lived in a one-bedroom apartment—a bachelor pad, essentially. Adding Alisa to it. Fine, he could handle that. It made the most sense since they were mates, but their baby?

That would be a stretch. So they were still deciding on whether to move out of the city and to the mountain address to raise their little dragon or get a bigger apartment.

Decisions, decisions.

In the meantime, his mother had come to stay with them. The already cramped situation became a thousand times worse. Though it was sort of necessary.

Since Alisa's mother and grandmother had passed, Sonya was elated to step up and midwife for Alisa. It'd been a difficult five weeks without the family she'd been raised with. Declan welcomed the support while Alisa mourned.

Throwing a wrap on the bed, Declan let out a huff. "Okay, time to go," he announced, turning his attention to Alisa.

"Sonya, are you sure you don't want to come? They'll have enough for one more person," Alisa offered sweetly.

Smiling warmly, Declan's mother shook her head ever so slightly. "You two enjoy your family. Someone needs to organize this mess before the egg arrives."

Glancing around, Declan snickered. There was no way to rearrange any of it to make the space more functional. They were bursting at the seams. What they needed to do was haul shit up north.

Tomorrow. He vowed that tomorrow he'd start emptying the apartment. "Just make sure, in your organizing, you don't mess up our system."

"System?" the women balked in unison.

"Yes!" he said, exasperated. "The stuff on this side is for Manhattan." He gestured to his right. "The stuff over there is for the mountain house. We need to keep it straight so we don't get confused."

They shared a look of skepticism.

He narrowed his eyes. "You fucked it up already, didn't you?"

"We still need to figure out crib or co-sleeping." Alisa changed the subject abruptly, confirming his suspicion.

"With the egg?" Declan asked.

"Yes!" Alisa said on a laugh.

"I've always been told the more time you spend warming your egg with your own body, the better," Sonya offered. "After I had lain, I wore my egg around the house and slept with it at night."

Declan arched a brow. "Weren't you afraid you'd break it?"

The thought of rolling over and squashing his egg gave him a shiver. Imagining the cracking sound was too much for him. He tried to shake it off, but the idea had already wormed its way into his mind.

She sniggered. "Of course not. The shell is quite thick during the brooding weeks. It thins as you get closer to hatching day. So it's perfectly fine, if not preferred."

Declan blinked a few times. He needed to get away from this conversation so the image would stop replaying in his head. "Seriously, we need to go."

Alisa

Alisa's father and his mate, Aimee, had the most extravagant apartment Alisa had ever seen. There was a foyer, a library, dining room, expansive kitchen, a den, three bedrooms, two bathrooms, and one half-bath. All of it decorated to perfection.

Between the gorgeous art on the walls, the fine furniture, and expensive-looking tchotchkes, the entire atmosphere screamed decadence. Alisa had been there a few times for dinners over the last few weeks, but she still felt somewhat out of place.

Not that it gave off a museum vibe or anything. The apartment was quite warm and welcoming. It just didn't feel like her home. It would take some getting used to.

She sat on a sofa in the den beside Declan. Fletcher and Duncan were across from her, and Gideon, at the bar, made drinks for the men.

Shifting in her seat, she tried to get comfortable. Definitely an impossibility considering she'd ballooned to the size of a house in the last two weeks.

Inhaling deeply, she reminded herself this was her surviving family and that should put her at ease despite her physical state.

As Gideon handed out half-filled glasses of scotch whiskey to his father, brother, and Declan, Alisa pushed herself off the couch.

"You okay?" Declan asked, his voice laced with concern.

"Yeah," she assured him with a wink.

Alisa rested a hand on the shelf that was her swollen belly. Moving around had gotten difficult the last two weeks. She looked like a nine-month pregnant human woman. Thankfully, she wouldn't have to endure the pregnancy that long.

"I'm just going to see if I can help set the table or something."

Declan nodded.

Alisa wasn't the best cook in the world. She could burn water if given the opportunity. So, she did her best to stay out of the way in the kitchen, but she still wanted to assist. Besides, if she sat on that sofa another ten minutes, she'd fall asleep.

The men were discussing jewelry business. There was nothing more boring than talking shop. Especially since Alisa wasn't a part of it.

Waddling her way through the dining room, she found the table had been impeccably set with fine china, a gorgeous floral centerpiece, and cute little place cards. Aimee had this homemaker thing down. Alisa might have to take lessons.

Her back twinged and Alisa flinched. She couldn't fathom how humans survived a nine-month pregnancy. It sure as shit wasn't for her.

Just as she was about to head for the swinging door to the kitchen to offer to clean the pots and pans, Ella came through carrying a steaming plate of green vegetables.

"Oh!" Startled, the human stopped in her tracks before colliding with Alisa. "Sorry. Didn't know you were there."

Zooming around Alisa, Ella went to the table and put the bowl down.

"Hot plate," she commented before resting her hand on a chair. "Do you mind if I ask you a few questions?"

Alisa smiled and rubbed the small of her back, trying to ease the pain throbbing there. "Sure, go for it."

"So, Gideon wants kids. I'm not sure we are ready. I just—" She glanced toward the door to the kitchen and then back to Alisa. "I'm a little scared about the whole pregnancy thing. I mean, I knew I didn't want to be pregnant if I had married a human, but a dragon?"

Her eyes widened when she realized she might have offended Alisa.

"No offense." She waved her hands in the air as though to fan her words away.

Alisa giggled. "Really, it's okay. I understand it could be quite frightening."

Nodding, Ella swallowed audibly before continuing. "I just, I wasn't sure who to ask about it. It feels weird talking to Gideon's mom since I only met her a few months ago. Not that I've known you that long or anything," Ella rambled as she picked nervously at her nails. "But you're kind of my age, so I guess it's less awkward." She chewed on her bottom lip.

Alisa did her best not to smile too much in the face of Ella's discomfort.

Finally, Ella flailed her arms out and came out with it. "How does it work?"

"Um, for you or for me?" Alisa asked as she tried to sort it in her head.

"I understand how it would work for me but for dragons."

True. Alisa's cheeks heated as she blushed. Of course, Ella was familiar with how humans reproduced. Why would she need Alisa to explain it?

Clearing her throat and her thoughts, she started at the beginning.

"Once you are fertilized, it takes six weeks for an egg to mature in the mother. Then you lay it." Alisa ran her hand in circles around her swollen stomach. She didn't think she had to explain how fertilization occurred. That bit was pretty universal.

Ella nodded. "Six weeks? That's it? I'd only have to be pregnant for six weeks?"

Alisa nodded and pointed to her giant belly. "Yep."

"Then what happens? I mean, with the egg?"

"Once it's laid, you need a nest to keep it warm. You should turn the egg frequently so the baby doesn't get like a flat head or a tiny leg or something." Alisa shrugged. "After about another six weeks, it hatches."

Ella bit her lip and leaned over the chair toward Alisa. "As a human baby?"

"Oh. No." Alisa shook her head. "It'll be a tiny dragon at first. They need the little beak thing to crack the shell. After about an hour, the scales shed, and the baby will appear human. We keep the scales so we can make the ink for a cloaking tattoo. It's how humans don't see us in dragon form."

Ella's eyes widened. Alisa wasn't so sure that was a good thing.

"Wow," she said on a heavy breath. "That is a lot to process."

Alisa grinned. "You are aware, if you choose to have kids with Gideon, you won't have to endure that. It will be a normal human pregnancy. Your eggs aren't dragon. They're human. So, while you may be able to produce a dragon, you won't have a dragon pregnancy."

Ella slumped a little. "Oh."

Alisa couldn't be sure if it was in relief or disappointment.

"I kinda liked the whole six weeks thing," Ella commented. "But like, how big is the egg?"

Alisa chuckled. "I haven't a clue, baby-sized. It's not that much larger than a human newborn. So, I guess the same."

Shaking her head, Ella thrummed her fingers on the back of a chair. "I really have to think on this."

"Talk to Gideon. I'm sure he will listen."

Ella's lips thinned and she nodded.

"Can I get help with the carrots and potatoes?" Aimee called from the kitchen. "I need someone to cut the mutton."

Alisa glanced over her shoulder before returning her focus to Ella.

"I'll handle the sides if you tell Duncan to cut the meat," Ella offered.

"It'll be okay when your time comes," Alisa said. "You don't have to rush it, and I'm sure Aimee will hold your hand through it. I will too."

Ella smiled warmly. "Thanks."

The smell of fresh mutton and all the fixings had Alisa's mouth watering. She had never seen such an elaborate spread. Especially for a random Sunday. It wasn't even a holiday. The Hayes had gone all out.

Seated with Declan to her right and Duncan at the head of the table to her left, Alisa tried to absorb the positive family energy swirling around the table. Even her dragon was content and slept peacefully within her mental confines.

Across from Alisa sat Gideon, with Ella beside him. Fletcher, the youngest of Duncan's children, was across from Ella. Duncan was positioned at the head of the table with Aimee at the foot. This was her new family. She'd had such a small one growing up, so this large group would take some getting used to.

As they passed the food around the table, Alisa's mind wandered to her grandmother.

Once Josephine had stripped Alisa's grandmother of her life essence, she'd aged exponentially. She was a husk of the vibrant woman she once was. Her hair had thinned and gone white. Her skin paled and wrinkled.

As a shifter, she'd didn't mature like humans. So Alisa never knew her true age. As a child, when she asked, her grandmother would smile and tell her, "It's just a number that doesn't matter." So, it was a surprise to learn she was actually one hundred and fifty-five years old. She looked to be in her fifties. That shifter healing ability was no joke. Unfortunately, she'd lost it in her sacrifice to Josephine.

Her frail appearance had unsettled Alisa. She'd never rid the image from her mind. At least she had it, though. She'd never had the opportunity to say goodbye to her mother. She left one day and just never came back.

Thankfully, Alisa had the chance with her grandmother at the mountain house. Her final day floated through Alisa's mind, and tears welled in her eyes.

It'd been bittersweet. Her grandmother was ready to go. She said she'd done all she wanted in life—raised Alisa and seen her happy with her mate. With the curse lifted, she could finally leave the mortal plane in peace. Her only regret was that she hadn't done it in time to save Alisa's mom.

Though Alisa wasn't sure that would've been possible. Her mother had gone mad from the loss of her chosen mate and didn't have faith she'd ever find a true one. The curse probably skewed her perception about it being a reality. While her mother's actions weren't justified, Alisa could understand them.

In doing so, the acceptance of her mother's actions allowed her to not only forgive her mother but also make sense of why her father stayed away so long.

"Are you okay?" Declan whispered as he placed a reassuring hand on her thigh.

Nodding, Alisa sniffled and swiped at the tears. "Hormones."

Her mate glanced around the table. They were doing their best not to obviously stare, but they definitely noticed her crying.

He licked his lips and met her gaze again. He squeezed her leg slightly. "Grandma?" he mouthed.

"That reminds me," Gideon announced, ruining their moment and drawing everyone's attention to him as he stood and gestured to Declan.

"Now?" Ella chided him.

He waved her away.

"I made something for you, Alisa. Consider it a welcome to the family gift." He beamed with pride.

Alisa glanced at Declan. Had he been told about this?

The smug grin he tried to hide indicated he definitely knew.

Then he offered her a rectangular, flattish black velvet box. She furrowed her brows as she accepted it. "What is this?"

His smile grew wider.

Carefully, she flipped open the lid and gasped at the oval locket inside. Fancy filigree decorated the silver-toned metal strung on a thin chain.

"It's made of tungsten. So it's crazy durable," Gideon explained.

"Open it," Declan urged.

Alisa gingerly fingered the beveled edge before finding the snap. Once she popped it open, she covered her mouth, but the gasp came out anyway. New tears welled in her eyes as her heart exploded with appreciation.

"I asked Gideon to make it," Declan explained. "When we were in the mountains, I found pictures of your grandma and your mother. It's unfair they can't be with you or the baby. So, I wanted you to always have them near."

She couldn't handle it. Tears streamed down her face, but she stifled the sobs. She met Declan's hopeful expression, but had no words.

"Do you like it?"

She did her best to speak, but jumbled gibberish was all she had. So, instead, she nodded vigorously.

"Can I put it on you?" he asked.

Again, she nodded.

"And that's not all," Gideon proclaimed.

Listening, Alisa turned, lifted her hair, and let Declan put the necklace on her.

"I made one for your egg too. So when it's old enough, it can carry them with it as well. I will do the same for every egg you lay. That's my gift for my sister," Gideon announced before he sat in his seat, satisfied.

There was no restraint now. The floodgates opened, and Alisa blubbered as she wrapped her arms around her mate.

While she lost a lot by coming to Manhattan, what she found was unimaginable. Her definition of family had definitely grown. Her outlook on her future was far brighter than Alisa had ever imagined it could be.

AUTHOR'S NOTE

Thank you for enjoying this journey with me and my characters. Authors love reviews. If you enjoyed this book, please consider leaving a review on Goodreads or your website of choice.

If you would like to be the first to hear about my latest news, please click here to sign up to my author newsletter. I send them out periodically for updates on my new releases, book recommendations, special offers, and/or exclusive content. I'm actively working on **Giving the Dragon Water**, the sequel to **Giving the Dragon Ice**. So stay tuned for updates.

Social Media

Find me on social media!

TikTok: https://www.tiktok.com/@authorvictoriajayne

Facebook: https://www.facebook.com/victoria.jayne.7982

Instagram: https://www.instagram.com/authorvictoriaj/

X (Formerly Twitter): https://twitter.com/AuthorVictoriaJ

Goodreads: https://www.goodreads.com/author/show/18610623.Victoria_Jayne

Bookbub: https://www.bookbub.com/profile/victoria-jayne

Books By Victoria Jayne

While you're waiting, feel free to check out some of my other books:

The Prophecy Trilogy:

The Witch of the Prophecy

The Wolf of the Prophecy

The Vampire of the Prophecy

Have you read the Odin's Fury Motorcycle Club Series?

Jacob

Sparrow

Dash

Gingersnap

Mooky

Blue

Elemental Dragon Series

Giving the Dragon Fire

Giving the Dragon Ice

Giving the Dragon Water (Coming Soon)